JOUSTING
WITH
THE DEVIL

© 2014 The American Chesterton Society
Printed in the United States of America
Cover illustration by Nicholas Blicharski
Cover and Interior design by Ted Schluenderfritz
LCCN: 2014944519
ISBN: 978-0-9744495-5-5

JOUSTING WITH THE DEVIL

CHESTERTON'S BATTLE WITH THE FATHER OF LIES

ROBERT WILD

ACS BOOKS

To Stratford Caldecott
A great Chestertonian, a great Catholic, and a great person

Knight of the Holy Ghost
Wisdom his motley, Truth his loving jest;
The mills of Satan keep his lance at play,
Pity and innocence his heart at rest.[1]

[1] Poem by Walter de la Mare on the service sheet for Chesterton's funeral.

"This is God's universe all right,
but there is the enemy."

Letter to W.R. Titterton

It is that the exorcist towers above the poet and even the prophet; that the story between Cana and Calvary is one long war with demons. He understood better than a hundred poets the beauty of the flowers of the battle-field; but he came out to battle. And if most of his words mean anything they do mean that there is at our very feet, like a chasm concealed among flowers, an unfathomable evil.

—G.K. Chesterton, *The New Jerusalem*

"In your book just published you tell us 'what is wrong with the world.' As I haven't read the book yet, would you mind telling me what is wrong?"

"The Devil."

(Interview with Chesterton in *Los Angeles Times*, August 18, 1910)

"The finding and fighting of positive evil is the beginning of all fun—and even of farce."

G.K. Chesterton, *The Flying Inn*

TABLE OF CONTENTS

INTRODUCTION
The Battle with the Dragon ... xiii

PREFACE ... xvii

CHAPTER ONE
"I Know the Unknown God"
CHESTERTON AND EVIL ... 1

CHAPTER TWO
"The Devil Made Me Do It"
CHESTERTON PUTS ON HIS ARMOR ... 35

CHAPTER THREE
"I Am Not Proud of Knowing the Devil"
THE ENCOUNTER ... 53

CHAPTER FOUR
THE HOLY WAR AND THE BALL AND THE CROSS ... 89

CHAPTER FIVE
THE FEARFUL AND HATEFUL ANTICHRIST
OF BENSON AND SOLOVIOV ... 121

CHAPTER SIX
GEORGE MACDONALD, EVIL, AND THE DEVIL ... 137

AFTERWORD ... 155

INTRODUCTION
The Battle with the Dragon

Satan is real. That's the first thing. The second thing should then be obvious: Satan is horrible. But the third thing may not be obvious: Satan is also ridiculous. But he is the only ridiculous thing that must be taken seriously.

This book explores G.K. Chesterton's encounter with the reality that is Satan. Whether or not you are familiar with Chesterton, you will be surprised at how familiar Chesterton is with this subject. Though he seems to have an intuitive sense of truth whatever his subject matter, when Chesterton writes about the Devil, he knows what he is talking about for more than intuitive reasons because his wisdom is supplemented by personal experience. And therein lies the surprise.

Chesterton is certainly known for his jollity, but also for his jousting. He set the tone with his first book of essays, *The Defendant*, establishing himself as a fighter, but a fighter on the side that is being attacked. He is one who defends the good when it is attacked by the bad, the normal when it is attacked by the abnormal, the princess when she is attacked by the dragon. He next made his name as a defender of orthodoxy. And a decade after he wrote a book by that name, he explained the significance of that word: "Orthodoxy never stood more for normality than in affirming that evil and not good is the usurper in the universe."[1]

Satan is the usurper in the universe, trying to rule what is not his to rule. The universe is not his; he did not make it. The Devil cannot *make* anything but can only destroy, he does not satisfy but can only tempt, he cannot impart wisdom, only doubt. Says Chesterton: "I could fancy that men drew the Tempter with the curves of a serpent because they can be twisted into the shape of a question mark."[2]

Why is it that we are often drawn to doubt, drawn to the Devil? The Devil is the one who will not subject himself to God, but who tries to take the place of God. "The Devil is he who says he is God. That is, he is one who says that his functions are infinite and cannot be judged."[3] That is the great temptation, to think that we can do whatever we want and not suffer any consequences for it.

It is a reality we constantly deny. We try to snake our way around it. We have substituted the Beast for the Devil and in the process convinced ourselves that the idea of the Devil is a fancy that comes from a beast, a beast that is merely myth. "It is the learned professor's point that the dragon evolved into the devil, but I think it far better psychology, as well as theology, to say that the devil took the form of the dragon."[4]

Chesterton gives a much better account of where the Dragon comes from:

---

[1] *New Witness*, May 17, 1917.

[2] *Illustrated London News*, January 27, 1917.

[3] *Daily Herald*, May 31, 1913.

[4] *The Observer*, September 14, 1919.

Introduction

There is a certain conception of the place of evil in life which I will call, by way of convenient symbol, the conception of St. George and the Dragon. The Dragon is bigger than St. George. He may look big enough to fill the world; but he is not the world; nor, above all, did he make the world. The stars are not the sparks from his flaming mouth, nor the clouds the smoke from his nostrils. The shadow of him may be big enough to blot out the world; but he is only a big blot on the world. The very effort to clear him away implies that there is something to be cleared. The stars, the air, the abstract truths, being itself and the breath of life, these exist anterior to and apart from the largest dragon; and exist in a sort of primordial innocence. This idea exists as an instinct in all healthy and hopeful attacks upon evil. But this idea as a philosophy is not identical with all philosophies. It is not the same as the pessimist philosophy, in which the dragon is the creator of all, who has only created St. George as a clockwork doll to play with and to break. It is not the same as the optimist philosophy, which explains away the dragon merely as the shadow of St. George; the long fantastic shadow of himself that gets on his nerves at twilight. It is not the same as a sort of Buddhist philosophy, which sees the evil only in the fact that the man and the monster are two things and not one; and thinks that all will be well when one of them swallows the other; the begging being rather on the dragon. It is not even the same as a promethean progressive philosophy, of something being evolved that will educate and improve an indifferent universe; or in other words the dragon is St. George's grandmother, but that he will be sufficiently enlightened to teach his grandmother. It is something quite different from all these, as we find if we attempt to define it; but whenever we are most sane we act upon it. I do not say that the more heroic heathens did not act upon it, before it was formed; they did. I do not say that the more healthy agnostics do not now act on it without defining it; they do. But I say this; that the more we do attempt to define it, the more we analyse it logically and state it lucidly, the more exactly we distinguish it from other moods of other minds, the more closely we shall find it approximating to the most dogmatic and disputed parts of what was called the theology of the Dark Ages; the nearer we shall come to the whole strange story of the treason of the archangel, of his betrayal of a divine plan, of his relative success and his ultimate failure. The shortest way of stating it is that evil is a tyranny, but it is also a temptation. Millions even in modern times act on that normal morality; millions do not reduce it to any philosophy; but if it is reduced to any philosophy it must be to this and no other.[5]

Chesterton rises above platitudes and even niceties and plunges into profound theology. That is the other surprise: that this journalist, this jouster, should oppose evil to its face and tell the eternal truths so plainly and so pointedly for the daily reader of throwaway newspapers. The Father of Lies would like us to think that truth evolves and even evaporates. But Chesterton's words survive because truth does not change, and truth is our only weapon against the lie.

As this book demonstrates, G.K. Chesterton is still swinging his sword. The horrible thing must be ridiculed, that is, it must be put in its place. But the battle to defeat the Dragon is serious business indeed.

—DALE AHLQUIST

---

[5] *New Witness*, October 8, 1920.

PREFACE

"We are Coming Out of the Desert"
— St. Anthony of Beaconsfield

In one sense this present book is a complement to my previous title *The Tumbler of God: Chesterton as Mystic*.[1] In that book I attempted to demonstrate that one of the main sources of G.K. Chesterton's sense of joy and wonder was a genuine mystical grace that enabled him to experience everything coming forth at every moment from the creative hand of God. For those not very familiar with Chesterton, or who have a rather superficial knowledge of his writings, they could have the impression that he didn't see any evil in the world. However, to correct such a notion, I want to emphasize in this book his belief in, and pugnacious battle with, *the devil*. Of course, he also believed in the evil present in the human heart, and in the "problem of evil" which philosophers try to explain. These last two have been treated in Mark Knight's *Chesterton and Evil*,[2] and we will be considering some of his insights below. My emphasis is explicitly on Satan.

In my research for this book I have often found that treatment of the devil in major works about Chesterton often lacking. For

---

[1] In Canada, *The Tumbler of God* (Justin Press: Ottawa, Ontario, 2012). Outside Canada (Angelico Press: Brooklyn, New York, 2013).

[2] Mark Knight, *Chesterton and Evil* (Fordham University Press: New York, 2004).

example, we have all profited very much from Aidan Nichols' *G.K. Chesterton, Theologian*;[3] and an increasing number of people will delight in Ian Ker's recent biography, *G.K. Chesterton*.[4] The following is not a criticism but a comment: there is no treatment at all in these books about the devil. One cannot cover all the bases in one book, but such omissions encouraged me to pursue the study of this topic. At the end of *Chesterton and Evil*, a book that you would think might have some treatment of the devil, Mark Knight, the author, says: "The response to evil that Chesterton constructs is multifaceted and comprehensive."[5] In my reading I have found that often the existence and influence of the devil is one of the "facets" omitted. Knight himself hardly treats the devil at all.

A very important and timely exception to the absence, or minimal mention, of Satan in the above-cited books occurs in Dale Ahlquist's excellent *The Complete Thinker: The Marvelous Mind of G.K. Chesterton*. In his Fourth Chapter "The Problem of Evil," Ahlquist's quote from Chesterton will be an excellent introduction to my theme. Speaking of the common man, Chesterton wrote:

> Something tells him that the ultimate idea of a world is not bad or even neutral; staring at the sky or the grass or the truths of mathematics or even a new-laid egg, he has a vague feeling like a shadow of that saying of the great Christian philosopher, St. Thomas Aquinas, 'Every existence, as such, is good.' On the other hand, something else tells him that it is unmanly and debased and even diseased to minimise evil to a dot or even a blot. He

---

[3] Aidan Nichols, O.P. *G.K. Chesterton, Theologian* (Darton, Longman and Todd: London, 2009).

[4] Ian Ker, *G.K. Chesterton, A Biography* (Oxford University Press: Oxford, 2011).

[5] Knight, pp. 149-50.

realises that optimism is morbid. It is, if possible, even more morbid than pessimism. These vague but healthy feelings, if he followed them out, would result in the idea that *evil is in some way an exception but an enormous exception; and ultimately that evil is an invasion or yet more truly a rebellion.* He does not think that everything is right or that everything is wrong, or that everything is equally right and wrong. But he does think that right has a right to be right and therefore a right to be there; and wrong has no right to be wrong and therefore no right to be there. It is the prince of the world; but it is also a usurper.[6]

Ahlquist comments: "Evil is an invasion. It is a rebellion. G.K. Chesterton says that he believed in the existence of the devil before he believed in God."[7] He then goes on to discuss the famous incident of "the diabolist" which I will also consider below.

Most of Chapter Four of Chesterton's *Autobiography* concerns his early encounter with evil and the dark side of the supernatural world.[8] His belief in the devil, and in the reality of evil in the human heart, were essential catalysts, both in clarifying who and what the enemy was, and in giving the battle the clang of reality and purpose. The poem by Walter de la Mare, cited at the beginning, is a significant confirmation of how some of his close friends understood that his battle was very much concerned with *Satan*, and that this was an essential aspect of his thinking and writings.

---

[6] *The Everlasting Man*, quoted by Dale Ahlquist, *The Complete Thinker* (Ignatius Press: San Francisco, 2012), pp. 57-58.

[7] *Ibid.*, p. 58.

[8] Although he said in 1906 (*Daily News*, Aug. 11) that "I believe in the supernatural as a matter of intellect and reason, not as a matter of personal experience," I don't believe this was true! The thesis of my book, *The Tumbler of God*, seeks to demonstrate that he received a mystical grace, which is an experience; and we shall see that his dabbling with the Ouija board was surely an experience of the dark side of the supernatural.

The theme running through this present book, and the inspiration that fueled it, is my belief that Chesterton is a new desert father, like St. Anthony the Great, immortalized by St. Athanasius in his *Life of Anthony*. No doubt my comparison may strike you—if you know anything about St. Anthony—as quite a preposterous and pretentious way of thinking about Chesterton. The reflections offered in this book are an attempt to justify, to some extent, this association of Chesterton with St. Anthony.

I've had the good fortune, during my life, to spend a fair amount of time in solitude, as a Trappist, as a Carthusian, and for many years as a poustinik in the Madonna House community (someone who lives in a little cabin called a poustinia). I mention these biographical details because I came to have a great love and reverence for the desert mothers and fathers who have transmitted to us some of the deepest wisdom the world has ever known. They have given us very profound insights into human nature, the spirit of the gospel, and especially to spiritual combat. They will always be for me one of the wisdom sources for my life with God.

Very simply, over the years, as I read Chesterton, I found in his writings also most profound insights about our relationship with God; and about other areas of life which the desert mothers and fathers never treated. Chesterton never wrote treatises on "the spiritual life." Actually he abhorred the word "spiritual." His charism was to give a faith perspective upon the whole of reality. He doesn't write like a desert father about "the spiritual life," but the truths he sees with his "eyes of faith" are equally profound, at least they are for me.

Chesterton ends his play "Temptation of St. Anthony" (1925) thus:

Time: You mean the New Religions do not tempt you?

Anthony: I mean I am waiting for them.

Time: Do you mean to suggest as a general criticism that the New Religion....

Anthony: [his voice ringing like a trumpet] *Mine* is The New Religion. We have waited nearly two thousand years and still its name is The New Religion. All this litter of old rags and bones you have swept in front of me is alone enough to prove that the Faith is the last thing of any importance that has happened in the world. I admit we have waited long for something new. I admit in that sense that the creed is something old. But it is newer than calling up ghosts or dancing without clothes, or healing people with spells, or believing in the transmigration of souls, or making up legends about men who lived to be hundreds of years old. It is newer than Egyptian mummies and Asiatic idols and omens and superstitions and dreams.

Go and tell your host [the devil] and your friends and all the cities of the heathens that *we* are coming out of the desert with a New Religion.[9]

After twenty years in the desert Anthony came out to teach others what he had learned. My contention is that Chesterton has emerged from the desert of the modern world—not having fasted as much as Anthony!—to proclaim the "New Religion" of the gospel of Christ in a powerful and ringing way, as did the desert dwellers of the early centuries. As a rather stocky journalist we may not exactly classify his kind of life-style with the asceticism of the desert dwellers. But could we not possibly think of him as a St. Anthony of Beaconsfield for modern times?

---

[9] *The Collected Works of G.K. Chesterton*, Vol. XI (Ignatius Press: San Francisco, 1989), p. 213.

And isn't it significant that Chesterton puts into the mouth of St. Anthony how he (Chesterton) understands his own apostolate: to proclaim to the modern world, which is being bombarded by all the "new religions," the gospel that has been forgotten? Did he see at least something of the *spirit of Anthony in himself*? Was St. Anthony one of his muses who influenced his own self-understanding?

If most people know anything at all about St. Anthony, they know, especially from the famous painting of Hieronymus Bosch, about the terrible temptations he suffered from the devils. "Satan's strategy was to awaken in Anthony memories of the things he once cherished: the bonds of kinship, such as those with his sister, or the satisfaction of food and life's other pleasures. With only his thoughts for companionship Anthony discovered the truth of the words of Jesus,[10] that the most lethal temptations arise not from without but from within the human breast. 'We have acquired a dark house full of war,' Anthony once said."[11] That the war is within our own house will be one of Chesterton's main approaches to "the problem of evil."

Much of Anthony's wisdom flowed from what he learned from these battles. And although we do not have very many famous sayings from Anthony, the testimony of his life was sufficient to make him the father of all the desert dwellers, and the recognized inspiration of this ascetic movement. It has been said that the *Life of St. Anthony* by St. Athanasius was, after the scriptures, the most influential book in the early centuries of Christendom.

Of course, I do not wish to compare Chesterton to St. Anthony; or, rather, yes, *I am going to compare him to St. Anthony*,

---

[10] Mark 7:20.

[11] Robert Louis Wilken, *The First Thousand Years: A Global History of Christianity* (Yale University Press, 2012), p. 101.

but will stop short of saying he is anyone *equal* to St. Anthony! But I *will* make a comparison: Chesterton, in his battle with the demons, emerged from the modern desert with astounding wisdom that have made him one of the greatest intellectual warriors for the gospel in modern times, and perhaps of all time. (And, as we shall see, it is important to fight erroneous ideas because, as Chesterton was fond of noting, they *cause* moral failings.)

Belief in Satan is part of our faith tradition. *The Catechism of the Catholic Church* states: "Behind the disobedient choice of our first parents lurks a seductive voice, opposed to God, which makes them fall into death out of envy. Scripture and the Church's Tradition see in this being a fallen angel, called, 'Satan' or the 'devil.' The Church teaches that Satan was at first a good angel, made by God: 'The devil and the other demons were indeed created naturally good by God, but they became evil by their own doing.'"[12]

Hans Urs von Balthasar writes about the existence of Satan. He first quotes a passage from Teilhard de Chardin, and then comments:

> (Teilhard): The quantity and the malice of evil *hic and nunc*, spread through the world, do not betray a certain excess, inexplicable to our reason, if to the *normal effect of evolution* is not added the *extraordinary effect* of some catastrophe or primordial deviation. Von Balthasar comments: Here looms the insoluble question of whether the 'excess' of suffering ascertained by the phenomenologist [Teilhard] has not something to do, even at the level of the subhuman world, with the 'principalities and powers' of which Paul speaks. Has it not something to do with the 'god of this world,' the 'prince' and

---

[12] *Catechism of the Catholic Church,* Second Edition, No. 391.

'ruler' of this world, whose original fall from God is responsible for the deep rent that goes from the bottom right up to the top—where it emerges as mankind's tragic history?[13]

A cardinal once said to St. John Paul II that some bishops don't believe in the devil. He said, "Then they don't believe in the gospel." Chesterton explicitly says—not surprisingly—that "Christ believed in the devils."[14] As far as the Catholic faith is concerned, it is not an optional belief.

A brief scriptural excursus may be helpful here. One of the petitions of the Our Father is "deliver us from evil."[15] The word used for "evil" is ambiguous, and thus we have various translations: the RSV: "but deliver us from evil"; the New International Version: "but deliver us from the evil one"; the New Jerusalem Bible: "but save us from the evil one."

The best commentaries interpret the Lord's Prayer in an eschatological sense: "'Lead us not into temptation' probably does not refer to the daily encounter with evil. The eschatological tone of the prayer suggests that the temptation meant is the great eschatological test, of which Matthew says (24:22) that no one could bear it unless it were abbreviated. 'Deliver us from evil': similarly, the eschatological catastrophe is very probably 'the evil' from which the Christian prays to be delivered in the final petition."[16]

However, it should be pointed out that it was the almost unanimous opinion of the early Church that it was the *Evil One* who was meant in the Lord's Prayer. And there are other

---

[13] Hans Urs von Balthasar, *Theodrama,* Theological Dramatic Theory IV: the Action (Ignatius Press: San Francisco, 1994), pp. 197-98.

[14] G.K. Chesterton, *The Everlasting Man* (Ignatius Press: San Francisco, 2008), p. 195.

[15] Matthew 6:13.

[16] *The Jerome Biblical Commentary*, p. 73.

passages in the New Testament that use the same word with the unambiguous meaning of the Evil One. For example, 1 John 2:13-14: "I write to you, young men, because you have overcome the evil one…; because you are strong, and the word of God lives in you, and you have overcome the evil one." The word is also unambiguous in some of the parables: "When anyone hears the message about the kingdom and does not understand it, the evil one comes and snatches away what was sown in his heart."[17] Thus, besides the accounts of exorcisms, the Evil One is also referred to as a person in the New Testament.

Belief in Satan was certainly part of the theology of the Fathers of the Church.

A quote from the great Origen will be very relevant to my theme.

Origen's *Against Celsus* is the greatest apologetical work of the early centuries. In discussing the problem or origin of evil with Celsus, Origen concludes his argument this way:

> No one, moreover, who has not heard what is related of him who is called 'devil,' and of his 'angels,' and what he was before he became a devil, and *how* he became such, and what was the cause of the simultaneous apostasy of those who are termed his angels, will be able to ascertain the origin of evils.
>
> But he who would attain to this knowledge must learn more accurately the nature of demons, and know that they are not the work of God so far as respects their demoniacal nature, but only in so far as they are possessed of reason; and also what their origin was, so that they became beings of such a nature, that while converted into demons, the powers of their mind remain. And if there be any topic of human investigation

---

[17] Matthew 13:19.

which is difficult for our nature to grasp, certainly the origin of evils may be considered to be such.[18]

Note that Origen acknowledges their ontological goodness: they had a being before they became devils; what they are now is not the work of God; they have reason; their origin is from God; the powers of their minds remain.

This teaching of Origen coincides with what Ralph Wood advised me after reading my manuscript: it's a distinction one should keep in mind throughout the present book. In a personal correspondence he wrote:

> I would urge you not to conflate the words 'personal' and 'positive' when treating the problem of evil. You will recall that St. Augustine adapted a strictly negative conception of evil from the neo-Platonists—namely, that evil is *privatio boni*, an absence or loss or lack of good. As such, it has no independence or positive existence but always remains parasitic, deriving its life negatively by living off its host. Yet precisely because evil is literally No-thing, it can assume all manner of states and conditions, including personal and demonic ones. Yet to give it positive status is to fall into the Manichean heresy of dualism, wherein God and the Demonic are set over against each other as contending positive and equal forces. Hence Chesterton's rightful seizure of the term 'nightmare': our experience of it could not be less terrifying, but finally it proves to be false, a chimera, a thing not real but imagined.[19]

As Origen taught, even Satan is ontologically good: he shares in existence, and in the powers to know and will. What he thinks

---

[18] Origen, *Contra Celsum*: Roberts, Alexander and James Donaldson, *Ante-Nicene Christian Library, Origen Contra Celsum*, Book IV, Chapter LXV.

[19] Personal communication to author, July 23, 2012.

and does are parasitic on his basic good qualities.

Belief in Satan has been on the wane in the western world for several centuries—what beliefs haven't been on the wane! On the other hand, there is also a growing awareness, a renewal of faith, in this aspect of the gospel that Jesus confirms for us.

There is now an international organization of exorcists, due mostly to the efforts of the famous Roman exorcist Gabriele Amorth. In Poland there is a new monthly magazine, *Egzorcysta*, dedicated entirely to exorcism. There have been several national conferences in the U.S. on exorcism; and more dioceses around the world once again have an official exorcist. It was the general practice before Vatican II for each diocese to have an exorcist. And when I was ordained it was still one of the minor orders before ordination. Chesterton alludes to this when he says some people only see Christ as an exorcist: "There is another theory [about Christ] that concentrates entirely on the business of diabolism and what it would call the contemporary superstition about demoniacs; as if Christ, like a young deacon taking his first orders, had gotten as far as exorcism, and never got any further."[20]

Belief in Satan and the existence of satanic cults and rituals is still very much with us. I went to a conference years ago on exorcism. A woman speaker got up and the first words out of her mouth were, "You are looking at the former high priestess of the satanic cult of the Eastern United States!"

John Allen Jr., probably the best Catholic reporter in the English-speaking world, outlines ten present trends in global Catholicism that will certainly be, in his estimation, part of the Church in the 21st century, and beyond. Belief in the devil is not one of his major trends, but it is one of the beliefs of

---

[20] *The Everlasting Man*, p. 197.

worldwide Christianity that will certainly endure. The reasons for this are not only because it is a traditional Christian belief, but even more so because most of Christianity will be south of the equator in Africa, South America and Asia. These are still "spiritual worlds" whose residents believe in spiritual realities such as miracles and the devil. Another major cause is the growth of Pentecostalism, the largest faith movement in the 20th and 21st centuries, whose belief in the devil and exorcism has already had an influence on the "renewal" of this belief in contemporary Catholicism.

Allen opens his book with this projected scene of 2025 where the first Nigerian pope, Victor IV "as he finishes the audience, descends to the first row of pilgrims, where, as he does each Wednesday, performs brief prayers of exorcism for visitors who have reported episodes of demonic possession."[21]

And this: "It does not tax the imagination to picture a future pope from the global South issuing an encyclical presenting Jesus Christ as the definitive answer to the 'spirits of this world.'"

Belief in the devil will not go away; interest in Chesterton will not go away. Please God, the relevance of this present book will not go away either as Chesterton can both help to confirm the Church's belief in this aspect of our faith, as well as give some discernment to global Catholicism on how to recognize the devil's influence and presence. Chesterton's pugnacious belief in the devil is another example of his witnessing strongly to one of the truths of the Catholic faith for the Church of our time.

Therefore, the main theme of this book is Chesterton's battle with evil spirits and with the lies they foster that are contrary to the gospel. Chapter One describes some aspects of Knight's treatment of evil in Chesterton's writings that will serve as a

---

[21] John Allen, Jr., *The Future Church* (Image: New York, 2009), pp. 13-14.

good background for my treatment of the devil. Chapter Two describes the fighting spirit that pervades all of Chesterton's writings. Chapter Three introduces his early encounters with the devil and the pervasiveness of this theme in his writings. Chapter Four treats his novel *The Ball and the Cross* that concerns his encounter with Professor Lucifer. Chapter Five compares *B&C* with two other apocalyptic novels of the same era—Robert Hugh Benson's *The Lord of the World* and Vladimir Soloviov's *The Story of the Anti-Christ*. Chapter Six reflects on the possible influence of George MacDonald on Chesterton's understanding of evil and the devil.

The word "prophet" is often used of Chesterton. A prophet is not so much someone who "sees" the future but who very deeply knows the present. He or she can see where present trends are heading. They "prophesize" that "if you don't change this course you are on, you are going to wind up in such and such a state." This was one of Chesterton's chief gifts: he saw deeply into the intellectual errors appearing on the horizon of his day and "predicted" that, if we don't change, this and this will happen. His "prophecies" are being proven right.

His belief in the devil is part of his prophetic message to the modern world. He believed in the reality of the devil in his day, and so he can make us aware of the reality of Satan as one of the perennial truths in the gospel for our times.

Chesterton's belief in the devil is an essential part of his prophetic mission. "If you don't believe in the devil you will lack the fighting spirit exemplified by Christ when he said to the disciples as they returned from their first mission: 'I have observed Satan fall like lightning from the sky.'[22] What is that

---

[22] Luke: 10:18.

but a shout of victory in a battle!"[23] If you don't believe in the devil you will attribute all the colossal evils in the world to human beings. Yes, we are capable of much evil, but there is an enormity of evil in some events that cannot be explained except by the presence of other evil forces besides human perversity. If you don't believe in the devil you will lack the vigilance that the Lord counsels in so many of his parables.

Belief in the devil is an essential part of Chesterton's message to the world, because it is an essential part of the gospel. "The whole point of Christianity is that a religion can no more afford to degrade its devil than to degrade its God."[24] Like many of Chesterton's phrases, this seems like an exaggeration. However, his point is that the whole truth of a religion must be accepted, and not just the nice, comforting aspects. Jesus thought we were capable of hearing the whole truth about reality, and that includes the devil.

Chesterton didn't often speak explicitly about the existence of the devil as he spoke about other tendencies that would arrive in the future. He simply believed in the devil, as does the Church, and wove belief in his battle with the satanic existence in and out of his writings. He didn't find this depressing: it was part of his faith understanding of reality. And in this also he is a prophet: he speaks this truth to every generation.

His poem, "To St. Michael, In Time of Peace," with its theme of the great archangel who "threwest down the Dragon" and the plea to "gird us with the secret of the sword," will form a fitting introduction to my topic:

Michael, Michael: Michael of the Morning,
Michael of the Army of the Lord,

---

[23] *The Everlasting Man*, p. 198.

[24] *The Everlasting Man*, p. 201.

Stiffen thou the hand upon the still sword, Michael,
Folded and shut upon the sheathed sword, Michael,
Under the fullness of the white robes falling,
Gird us with the secret of the sword.

When the world cracked because of a sneer in heaven,
Leaving out for all time a scar upon the sky,
Thou didst rise up against the Horror in the highest,
Dragging down the highest that looked down on the Most
    High:
Rending from the seventh heaven the hell of exaltation
Down the seven heavens till the dark seas burn:
Thou that in thunder threwest down the Dragon
Knowest in what silence the Serpent can return.

Down through the universe the vast night falling,
(Michael, Michael: Michael of the Morning!)
Far down the universe the deep calms calling
(Michael, Michael: Michael of the Sword!)
Bid us not forget in the baths of all forgetfulness,
In the sigh long drawn from the frenzy and the fretfulness
In the huge holy sempiternal silence
In the beginning was the Word.

When from the deeps of dying God astounded
Angels and devils who do all but die
Seeing Him fallen where thou couldst not follow,
Seeing Him mounted where thou couldst not fly,
Hand on the hilt, thou hast halted all thy legions
Waiting the Tetelestai and the acclaim,
Swords that salute Him dead and everlasting
God beyond God and greater than His Name.

Round us and over us the cold thoughts creeping
(Michael, Michael: Michael of the battle-cry!)
Round us and under us the thronged world sleeping
(Michael, Michael: Michael of the Charge!)
Guard us the Word; the trysting and the trusting
Edge upon the honour and the blade unrusting
Fine as the hair and tauter than the harpstring
Ready as when it rang upon the targe.

He that giveth peace unto us; not as the world giveth:
He that giveth law unto us; not as the scribes:
Shall he be softened for the softening of the cities
Patient in usury; delicate in bribes?
They that come to quiet us, saying the sword is broken,
Break man with famine, fetter them with gold,
Sell them as sheep; and He shall know the selling
For He was more than murdered. He was sold.

Michael, Michael: Michael of the Mustering,
Michael of the marching on the mountains of the Lord,
Marshal the world and purge of rot and riot
Rule through the world till all the world be quiet:
Only establish when the world is broken
What is unbroken is the word.[25]

---

[25] G.K. Chesterton, "To St. Michael in Time of Peace." This poem was first published in *The Legion Book* (London 1929), and again in *G.K.'s Weekly* (September 24, 1936). The poem also appeared in *The Chesterton Review*, Vol. XVI, No. 2, May 1990, Seton Hall University, South Orange, New Jersey.

CHAPTER ONE

"I Know the Unknown God"
CHESTERTON AND EVIL

Several years into the research for this manuscript I came across *Chesterton and Evil* by Mark Knight (mentioned in the Preface). My first thought was, "Oh no! Somebody's already written a book about Chesterton and the devil!" But upon reading the book my anxieties were put to rest. I was actually quite surprised—and relieved—that Knight hardly touches at all upon the part belief in a *personal devil* played in Chesterton's life and writings! He treats evil in some of the traditional philosophical ways—i.e., the *privatio boni*—and then examines, especially in the Father Brown Stories and the early novels—how Chesterton treats evil using various literary forms, for example, the grotesque. His book, therefore, will serve as one background for my treatment of the devil in Chesterton. I want to quote here, though, a rather lengthy passage from Knight about the devil. I start with this quote because, really, *it is the only passage where he deals explicitly with the devil.* I will mercifully omit all of the author's references as they are quite numerous:

> Chesterton's resistance to dualism and his corresponding insistence that all persons contain a mixture of good and evil

raise questions about the devil. Following Aquinas, Chesterton understood the devil as one who persuades people to sin, and in his poem 'The Aristocrat' Chesterton went along with the nineteenth-century inheritors of Faust in conceiving of Satan as a gentleman who promises good things but does not 'keep his word' (a man much like Wilde's Lord Henry). However, Chesterton's desire to avoid theological dualism left him in a similar quandary to Aquinas: How much and what sort of a role to assign to the devil? Despite the large number of references to the devil that can be found in the Father Brown stories, the references are openly metaphorical rather than literal attempts to account for the evil that transpires.

This explains why, despite Father Brown's acknowledgment in 'The Dagger with Wings' that 'all evil has one origin,' the story subsequently makes it clear that the 'man who is hounding us all to death' is not 'a hell-hound,' nor is his power 'from hell.' Many of the Father Brown stories go out of their way to explain the diabolic in human terms, as can be seen from Father Brown's insistence in 'The Miracle of Moon Crescent' that the blame is entirely human: 'You don't think the holy angels took him and hung him on a garden tree, do you? And as for the unholy angels—no, no, no. The men who did this did a wicked thing, but they went no further than their own wickedness.'[1]

Before commenting on Knight's interpretation, Chesterton's poem "The Aristocrat" will fit in nicely with the latter's understanding of the character of Satan:

The Devil is a gentleman and askes you down to stay

---

[1] Knight, pp. 46-47.

At his little place at What'sitsname (it isn't far away).
They say the sport is splendid; there is always something new,
And fairy scenes, and fearful feats that none but he can do;
He can shoot the feathered cherubs if they fly on the estate,
Or fish for Father Neptune with the mermaids for a bait;
He scaled amid the staggering stars that precipice the sky,
And blew his trumpet above heaven, and got by mastery
The starry crown of God Himself and shoved it on the shelf;
But the devil is a gentleman, and doesn't brag himself.

O blind your eyes and break your heart and hack your hand away,
And lose your love and shave your head; but do not go to stay
At the little place in What's its name where folks are rich and clever;
The golden and the goodly house, where things grow worse forever;
There are things you need not know of, though you live and die in vain,
There are souls more sick of pleasure than you are sick of pain;
There is a game of April Fool that's played behind its door,
Where the fool remains forever and April comes no more,
Where the splendour of the daylight grows drearier than the dark,
And life droops like a vulture that once was such a lark:
And that is the Blue Devil, that once was the Blue Bird;
For the Devil is a gentleman, and doesn't keep his word.[2]

Neither is this benign characterization of the devil foreign to popular culture. Here are the lyrics to a Bob Dylan song:[3]

---

[2] G.K. Chesterton, "The Aristocrat." Best Poems. Web. 27 Jun. 2014.

[3] Sent to me by my brother Jerry.

He got sweet gift of gab, he got harmonious tongue
He know every song of love that ever has been sung
Good intentions can be evil, both hands can be full of grease
You know that sometimes Satan come as a man of peace

Well, first he's in the background, then he's in the front
Both eyes are lookin' like they're on a rabbit hunt
Nobody can see through him, no, not even the chief of police
You know that sometimes Satan come as a man of peace

Well, he catch you when you're hopin' for a glimpse of the sun
Catch you when your trouble feel like they weigh a ton
He could be standin' next to you, the person that you'd notice least
I hear that sometimes Satan come as a man of peace.

I am not as competent as Knight to discuss whether or not all the references to "Satan, devilish, diabolical, hellish" and so on in the Father Brown stories are metaphorical. But I will offer a few comments.

In contrast to Knight's own metaphorical interpretations, it is interesting to note that, later on in the book he quotes one Frederick Crosson *re* the Father Brown methodology: "It is rather that the stories are not just stories of crimes in a legal or even a moral sense. The crimes they tell are of evil deeds, *deeds prompted by the Evil one* [emphasis mine], crimes not only against man but against God—and crimes which violate the soul of the actor himself."[4]

My own opinion is that, generally, Father Brown has the whole panoply of Catholic theology about evil behind his investigative mind, which includes the devil. I read the Father Brown stories that Knight cites. The references to the devil

---

[4] Knight, p. 41.

that I came across *do not in any sense seem metaphorical to me*. Like us, Father Brown may occasionally use phrases like, "the devil you say" or "what in the devil's name is that all about" or "it's a really hellish situation." But here are some quotes from the clerical detective about the devil that I think are not metaphorical:

> 'What the devil are you talking about,' said the doctor with a loud laugh.
> Flambeau spoke quietly to him in answer. 'The Father sometimes gets this mystic's cloud on him,' he said. 'But I give you fair warning that I have never known him to have it except when there was some evil quite near.'
> 'The Duke said, 'You shall not spell the first letter of what is written on the altar of the Unknown God.'[5]
> 'I know the unknown God,' said the little priest, with an unconscious grandeur of certitude that stood up like a granite tower. 'I know his name; it is Satan. The true God was made flesh and dwelt among us. And I say to you, wherever you find men ruled merely by mystery, it is the mystery of iniquity. If the devil tells you something is too fearful to look at, look at it. If he says something is too terrible to hear, hear it. If you think some truth unbearable, bear it. I entreat your Grace to end this nightmare now and here at this table.'[6]

"Unconscious grandeur of certitude" surely refers to a reality that the good Father believes in.

Consequently, after my brief perusal of these Father Brown stories, what I am somewhat capable to dispute is Knight's

---

[5] G.K. Chesterton, *The Complete Father Brown* (Penguin Books Ltd: Harmondsworth, England, 1981), p. 253.

[6] *Ibid.*, p. 92.

conclusion to his above quoted paragraph: "Father Brown's observation here, concurring as it does with Chesterton's own writings on free will, implies that the devil serves little function in Chesterton's explanation of the evil that occurs in the world."[7]

I must say that after a number of years working on this manuscript I found that opinion quite astonishing; and this book is my refutation of that opinion. Or rather, my subject can be seen as an important aspect of *Chesterton and Evil* that has hardly been considered at all in Knight's work.

Walter de la Mare did not mean that Chesterton was jousting with the *privatio boni* of the philosophers, or with a reality of only metaphorical significance! True to Catholic teaching, Chesterton did not attribute all evil to Satan; and with his rapier-like intellect he jousted with evil in all its forms. But my thesis is that he also did conscious battle with Satan. I do not say this was the absolute and most important center of all his battles, but it was very significant and an essential part of his understanding of the Holy War all Christians are waging. The existence of the devil and his possible influence in any situation was always at the back of his mind. That is what this book is about. But first some thoughts from Knight's helpful book that will serve as a background for my own study. (Quotes in this chapter are from Knight unless otherwise noted.)

Knight begins, in Part 1, by mentioning the superficial criticism of some people that I have alluded to, namely, that Chesterton was unaware of evil in the world. Quoting Charles Masterman: "Mr. Chesterton is convinced that the Devil is dead. A children's epileptic hospital, a City dinner, a suburban at home, a South African charnel camp, or any other examples

---

[7] Knight, p. 47.

of cosmic ruin fail to shake this blasphemous optimism." (This present book is an attempt to demonstrate that, for Chesterton, the devil was *not* dead.)

Knight endeavors to show that Chesterton's optimism was not simply a reaction to the well-documented pessimism of the age, but was meant to highlight the wonder of existence itself. "By arguing that the goodness of existence is prior to suffering, he seeks to locate evil as a secondary issue."[8] Chesterton was essentially a religious thinker, and so the existence of evil was certainly part of his faith.

Part 2 of Knight is entitled "The 1890's, Detective Fiction, and the Nature of Evil." In the early Father Brown stories Chesterton seeks to clarify the boundaries between good and evil that had become very blurred in his time. Impressionism was one of the chief muddling factors. The Father Brown genre "had the great advantage of being predicated on an attempt to confront and root out evil."

One of the differences between Chesterton's and Sherlock Holmes's methodology is significant for the former's

---

[8] I may be mistaken, but I think Chesterton would agree that the goodness of existence is primary, and suffering is a secondary issue. Here is one of the most oft-quoted insights of Chesterton, and one of my favorites: "There is at the back of all our lives an abyss of light, more blinding and unfathomable than any abyss of darkness; and it is the abyss of actuality, of existence, of the fact that things truly are, and that we ourselves are incredibly and sometimes incredulously real. It is the fundamental fact of being, as against not being; it is the unthinkable, yet we cannot unthink it, though we may sometimes be unthinking about it; unthinking and especially unthanking. For he who has realised this reality knows that it does outweigh, literally to infinity, all lesser regrets or arguments for negation, and that under all our rumblings there is a subconscious substance of gratitude. This is something much more mystical and absolute than any modern thing that is called optimism; for it is only rarely that we realise, like a vision of the heavens filled with a chorus of giants, the primeval duty of Praise." G.K. Chesterton, *Chaucer.* Quoted by Joseph Pearce, *Wisdom and Innocence: A Life of G.K. Chesterton* (Ignatius Press: San Francisco, 2004), p. 17.

understanding of an aspect of evil in the world: evil is also in the human heart. "Father Brown is keen to emphasize his empathy with the criminals that he pursues. This can be seen in 'The Secret of Father Brown' when Grandison Chace, having pressed the priest for an explanation of his methodology, receives the following shocking response: 'You see, I had murdered them all myself. So, of course, I knew how it was done.' Father Brown says his methodology is not a study of the man from the outside: 'I don't try to get outside the man. I try to get inside the murderer.'"

In the Father Brown stories Chesterton, who had an orthodox Catholic mind even before becoming Catholic, avoids both dualism (that there is a rival bad god), and monism ("that good and evil are merely aspects of a single universal structure.") Knight does a good job in pointing out how Chesterton navigates around these philosophical shoals in the detective stories.

And what is Chesterton's basic navigational compass? The classical doctrine from Augustine and Aquinas of *privatio boni*: "For Father Brown (and Chesterton) evil is not a substance in and of itself but rather a corruption of that which is good." As a theme in the stories Father Brown puts it this way in "The Dagger with Wings": "All things are from God; and above all, reason and imagination and the great gifts of the mind. They are good in themselves; and we must not forget their origin even in their perversion."

Part 3 is entitled "Creation and the Grotesque." Knight begins with many examples of how Chesterton mostly emphasized the goodness of creation in his fiction. This is Knight's background for discussing Chesterton's use of the grotesque to describe evil.

No one agrees on a definition of "grotesque." Knight outlines three ways he will examine Chesterton's use of this genre. I choose just one for consideration here—"the combination of comedy with terror." And even in this category Knight further distinguishes between "Chesterton's use of the grotesque as a description of strangeness and his use of the term as a means of describing something that is *deformed or corrupt.*" "Chesterton believed that the *strange* was part of God's original design, whereas the *deformed* was a result of sin. The deformed grotesque is more appropriate to capturing the evil that results from a Fallen Creation." This last category—the deformed grotesque—is more relevant for my purposes.

Knight cites several authors who suggest that Chesterton's use of the deformed grotesque was to avoid or deemphasize evil. Knight disagrees: But, for Chesterton, "the issue was not so much whether evil should be imagined but rather how it should be imagined without according it too much status. Even in its deformed variety the grotesque remains contingent on Creation. Existence is prior to distortion."

What is one of Chesterton's supreme examples of the distorted grotesque? It is Professor Lucifer in *The Ball and the Cross*. Quoting Cammaerts again: "The moralist has parted the sheep from the goats. As in the medieval picture, there is no subtle nuance between good and evil, and the devil is always painted black." One of the main themes of the novel is "that the world has become corrupted through deficient ideas and misplaced ideologies." The heart of my thesis in this present book is that the main work of the devil is to insinuate deficient ideas and false ideologies. It is these false conceptions that our modern St. Anthony of Beaconsfield is fighting in the caves of the modern mind.

Satan has a "deformed personality," and here are some of Chesterton's characteristics of Professor Lucifer as cited by Knight: "dreadful mirth"; "a cruel voice which always made all human blood turn bitter"; "the [Professor's] eyes were full of a frozen and icy wrath, a kind of utterly heartless hatred"; "thus we find him [the Professor] beaming at them all with a sinister benignity"; "Lucifer leapt upon him with a cry like a wild beast's." Professor Lucifer is Chesterton's description of the "deformed personality" of Satan.

In reference to Chesterton and the grotesque, Knight has an interesting quote from Bernard McElroy:

> In earlier art, the source of the grotesque was usually the external realm, natural or supernatural. In societies where men felt themselves to be at the day to day mercy of potent, malevolent spiritual powers, the grotesque often embodies that which, though invisible, was presumed to exist. But in the modern Western world, deeply aware of the rift between the external, objective world and the internal, subjective interpretation of it, the source of the grotesque has moved and is found in the fears, guilts, fantasies, and aberrations of individual psychic life. The modern grotesque is internal, not infernal, and its originator is recognized as neither god nor devil but man himself.[9]

Knight continues: "The traditional grotesque is based upon an external figure of evil, whereas in the modern grotesque evil is internalized. The story [B&C] quickly goes on to link this to the external embodiment of evil that Professor Lucifer presents."[10] In other words, according to this interpretation, Chesterton is an "earlier" artist, medieval even. Unlike some modern artists who may have the Professor symbolize the internal "fears, guilts, fantasies, and aberrations" of the psyches of his characters, Chesterton is writing about an *external personified*

---

[9] Knight, pp. 100-101.
[10] *Ibid.*

evil. (Some modern scripture scholars, who no longer believe in demons, now interpret the devils in the scripture as psychological phenomena.)

Part 4 is entitled "Nothingness, Solipsism, and the Grotesque." "*The Man Who Was Thursday* presents us with Chesterton's most profound and sustained use of the deformed grotesque. The protagonists find themselves unable to make sense of a world that appears to offer a closed, unintelligible system of thought." "The novel depicts evil that is pervasive and widespread."

And in his *Autobiography* Chesterton is more specific about *Thursday*: "The whole story is a nightmare of things, not as they are, but as they seemed to the young half-pessimist of the '90's." (I describe below more fully these nightmares.) Knight gives the name of "nothingness" to one aspect of evil Chesterton was struggling with: "The implication of the text at several points is that there is nothing outside or beyond the grotesque world represented." In short, there is nothingness beyond the nightmare. (Elsewhere Chesterton says that "where there is nothing, there is Satan.")[11]

The other demon in *Thursday* was solipsism: "The belief that there is no reality outside one's own thought. This was heavily shaped by his experiences of Impressionism while at the Slade School of Art. Describing these experiences in his *Autobiography*, he argued that Impressionism's subjectivity engendered the skepticism toward the external realm that culminated in his own feelings of isolation." Thus in *Thursday* he is experiencing, and giving literary form through the grotesque, to nothingness, solipsism, and loneliness.

I am not so much concerned here—which is the subject of

---

[11] G.K. Chesterton, *Utopia of Usurers*, "The French Revolution" (IHS Press: Norfolk, 2002).

Knight's book—with how Chesterton dealt with these demons *in literary forms*. My own specific purpose in the present book is to add that *the devil was also part of his faith understanding*, and often in the background of his thinking, but at times very explicit in his writing.

Knight entitles Part 5 "Confession, the Church, and the Problem of Evil." Only the sections on "The Free Will Defense" and "the Book of Job" are relevant for my purposes. Knight doesn't really treat here any new evils. Rather he expands on some of Chesterton's approaches, and other traditional Christian approaches to the "problem of evil."

Foremost among Chesterton's dealings with evil is the Free Will Defense which argues that God gave humanity free will and that the misuse of this free will allowed sin and evil to enter the world. Thus, all-pervasive in Chesterton's writings is our freedom. As he says in *Orthodoxy*: "But the point is that a story is exciting because it has in it so strong an element of will, of what theology calls free-will. You cannot finish a sum how you like. But you can finish a story how you like." And commenting also in *Orthodoxy* on his play *The Surprise*: "God had written, not so much a poem, but rather a play; a play he had planned as perfect, but which had necessarily been left to human actors and stage-managers, who had since made a great mess of it."

The Free Will Defense is a philosophical, rational attempt to explain the reality of evil. But Chesterton was not a rationalist; and ultimately this "problem of evil" does not admit of any explanation. Chesterton's comments on the Book of Job[12] emphasize this ultimate mystery about suffering: Job doubted everything until he finally doubted himself, that is, doubted his

---

[12] Cf. my treatment of Chesterton and Job in *The Tumbler of God*, Chap. 11.

ability to get his mind around why he was suffering. Ultimately he trusts God, even though this God gives no answer at all. "Though he slays me, yet will I trust him." Knight's conclusion to the book is a good way of ending this brief and very selective presentation of his study:

> In place of the popular caricatures of Chesterton as a lightweight and optimistic writer who was largely ignorant of suffering and pain, we find a writer who made a serious attempt to comprehend evil. At the heart of Chesterton's response to evil was an appeal to the Creation upon which evil is contingent. This appeal is strengthened by Chesterton's location of the doctrine of Creation alongside a series of other beliefs, including, most importantly, a version of the Free Will Defense that acknowledges the need for individuals to express their freedom in relation to a wider community. The response to evil that Chesterton constructs is multifaceted and comprehensive, and yet it does not claim to offer a definitive answer to evil.

I must say that I found in Knight's presentation many valuable insights from Chesterton—especially in the comments by Father Brown—that are very helpful intuitions into the problem of evil. But to repeat what I said in the Preface: *the facet of Satan is lacking in* Knight's multifaceted presentation of evil in Chesterton.

I close this section with one quote from *Orthodoxy* by Knight that I found most helpful: "The real trouble with this world of ours is not that it is an unreasonable world, nor even that it is a reasonable one. The commonest kind of trouble is that it is nearly reasonable, but not quite." It is this "almost reasonable" universe that led Gary Wills to speak of Chesterton's *riddling God*.

The Origins of Chesterton's Belief in the Devil

William Oddie's *Chesterton and the Romance of Orthodoxy: The Making of Chesterton, 1874-1908*,[13] is considered the best study of Chesterton's early development. Chapter Three, "Nightmare at the Slade," is of particular relevance for my topic. He spends several pages commenting on Chesterton's dedication of *Thursday* to his best friend E.C. Bentley. He finds in this dedication a very important turning point in Chesterton's thought. It will be helpful to quote the whole dedication, although some parts are very familiar:

> A cloud was on the mind of men, and wailing went the weather,
> Yea, a sick cloud upon the soul when we were boys together.
> Science announced nonentity and art admired decay;
> The world was old and ended; but you and I were gay;
> Round us in antic order their crippled vices came—
> Lust that had lost its laughter, fear that had lost its shame.
> Like the white lock of Whistler, that lit our aimless gloom,
> Men showed their own white feather as proudly as a plume.
> Life was a fly that faded, and death a drone that stung;
> The world was very old indeed when you and I were young.
> They twisted even decent sin to shapes not to be named:
> Men were ashamed of honour; but we were not ashamed.
> Weak if we were and foolish, not thus we failed, not thus;
> When that black Baal blocked the heavens he had no hymns
>   from us.
> Children we were—our forts of sand were even as weak as we,
> High as they went we piled them up to break that bitter sea.
> Fools as we were in motley, all jangling and absurd,
> When all church bells were silent our cap and bells were heard.

---

[13] (Oxford University Press: Oxford, 2008), pp. 114-115.

Not all unhelped we held the fort, our tiny flags unfurled;
Some giants laboured in that cloud to lift it from the world.
I find again the book we found, I feel the hour that flings
Far out of fish-shaped Paumanok some cry of cleaner things;
And the Green Carnation withered, as in forest fires that pass,
Roared in the wind of all the world ten million leaves of grass;
Or sane and sweet and sudden as a bird sings in the rain—
Truth out of Tusitala spoke and pleasure out of pain.
Yes, cool and clear and sudden as a bird sings in the grey,
Dunedin to Samoa spoke, and darkness unto day.
But we were young; we lived to see/ God break their bitter charms.
God and the good Republic come riding back in arms:
We have seen the City of Mansoul, even as it rocked, relieved—
Blessed are they who did not see, but being blind, believed.
This a tale of those old fears, even of those emptied hells,
And none but you shall understand, the true thing that it tells—
Of what colossal gods of shame could cow men and yet crash,
Of what huge devils hid the stars, yet fell at a pistol flash.
The doubts that were so plain to chase, so dreadful to withstand—
Oh, who shall understand but you; yea, who shall understand?
The doubts that drove us through the night as we two talked amain,
And the day had broken on the streets e'er it broke upon the brain.
Between us, by the peace of God, such truth can now be told;
Yes, there is strength in striking root and good in growing old.
We have found common things at last and marriage and a creed,
And I may safely write it now, and you may safely read.

The following passage from this chapter of Oddie's is worth quoting at length. It serves as an excellent statement of the theme of my whole book—Chesterton's pugnacious belief in Satan. (*Mansoul* is Bunyan's second spiritual allegory.)

> Now, we have moved on in no uncertain way. And it is at this point, it seems to me, that we find an important key to Chesterton's own feelings about those years in which he was coming to literary maturity. *It is not simply that the fin de siecle was a period in which men had gone mad: it was a time when they were possessed by a great evil, in which the city, like Mansoul, was besieged by the hosts of the devil.* [emphasis mine] And he continues, in the Bentley dedication—in dramatic and almost allegorical language which really does make one think of Bunyan—men were 'cowered' by 'colossal gods of shame'. They were filled with doubts 'dreadful to withstand'; it was a time in which 'huge devils hid the stars'.
>
> This is a language different from that of the humorous argumentation with which Chesterton was, in the early years of the new century, already fighting the culture wars of later decades. And yet it is here, I think, that we must look for the real origins of Chesterton's mature philosophy of life. *Chestertonian orthodoxy begins not simply with a perception of unorthodoxy, of intellectual incoherence or aberration, but with a vision of positive evil.* [emphasis mine] As he puts it in the *Autobiography,* 'I dug quite low enough to discover the devil; and even in some dim way to recognize the devil. At least I never, even in this first vague and skeptical stage, indulged very much in the current arguments about the relativity of evil or the unreality of sin. Perhaps, when eventually emerged as a sort of theorist, and was described as an Optimist, it was because I was one of the few people in that world of diabolism who really believed in devils.' This was a nightmare which faded with the light of day, but which remained with Chesterton to the end of his days, hidden but always there as an imaginative

and intellectual force.[14]

Here is one example of how the devil remained "an imaginative and intellectual force." Chesterton came across a writer praising modern advertising who said that good salesmanship made "everything in the garden beautiful." Chesterton wrote:

> There was only one actor in that ancient drama who seems to have had any real talent for salesmanship. He seems to have undertaken to deliver the goods with exactly the right preliminaries of promise and praise. He knew all about advertisement: we may say he knew all about publicity, though not at the moment addressing a very large public. He not only took up the slogan of Eat More Fruit, but he distinctly declared that any customers purchasing his particular brand of fruit would instantly become as gods. And as this is exactly what is promised to the purchasers of every patent medicine, popular tonic, saline draught or medicinal wine at the present day, there can be no question that he was in advance of his age. It is extraordinary that humanity, which began with the apple and ended with the patent medicine, has not even yet become exactly like gods. It is still more extraordinary (and probably the result of a malicious interpolation by priests at a later date) that the record ends with some extraordinary remarks to the effect that one thus pursuing the bright career of Salesmanship is condemned to crawl on his stomach and eat a great deal of dirt.[15]

Chesterton is speaking about how moderns use the new psychological jargon without knowing what it means. "Superiority Complex," for example: "For he has never thought about the

[14] Oddie, pp. 114-115.

[15] Quoted by Pearce, p. 365.

phrase he uses; he has only seen it in the newspapers. The new phrase is not in the newspapers; and he has never heard of it. But the much older and much more profound Psychology of the Christian Religion was founded on the very ancient discovery that a superiority complex was the beginning of all evil."[16] Satan was the first victim of the superiority complex.

I will briefly attempt to flesh out factors in Chesterton's personal makeup that contributed to what Oddie pinpointed as a "vision of positive evil" that ever remained to the end of his days. What were some of the deeper origins of this vision? I will describe three. The first is rather "mystical" and, I admit, my own interpretation: that he *was given a quasi-mystical grace* of an extraordinary awareness of the reality of evil. The second origin was his personal and philosophical problems that accentuated this awareness. The third was his actual encounter with evil spirits.

A "Mystical" Awareness of Evil?

In the last few years two articles have appeared in *The Chesterton Review* with the same title, "The Spirituality of Chesterton."[17] Significantly, and rather surprisingly, both articles—rather short—gave first place and prominence to the theme of this book! In the first, by Karl Schmude, after mentioning briefly the commonly cited positive aspects of Chesterton's character—"his innocence and goodness, his playfulness, his kindly character," and so on, he says this: "I am merely suggesting that there is

---

[16] G.K. Chesterton, *Sidelights on New London and Newer York, and Other Essays* (Dodd and Mead: New York, 1932), pp. 60-61. Quoted by Pearce, p. 407.

[17] Karl Schmude, "The Spirituality of G.K. Chesterton," *The Chesterton Review*, Vol. XXXII, Nos. 1 & 2, Spring/Summer 2006, Seton Hall University, South Orange N.J., 97-111; and George Bull, "The Spirituality of G.K. Chesterton," *The Chesterton Review*, Vol. XXVI. No. 4, November 2000.

another side of Chesterton that has become more significant, and more salient, in recent decades." He then presents insights from Jorge Luis Borges that especially attracted my attention. It was only after working on this present manuscript for several years that I first came across this insight by Borges. I think it is a penetrating reflection into one of the causes—and perhaps the deepest cause—of Chesterton's battle with evil.

> Borges saw in Chesterton dark strains and hints of horror. He thought that Chesterton represented 'the precarious subjection of a demoniacal will.' Beneath the surface sparkle of wit and optimism lurked a fear that the world is a depraved and diabolical place. Chesterton, argued Borges, 'restrained himself from being Edgar Allan Poe or Franz Kafka, but something in the makeup of his personality leaned towards the nightmarish, something secret, and blind, and central.'[18]

A continuation of that quote from Borges may be of interest: "Not in vain did he [Chesterton] repeat that the best book to come out of Germany was *Grimm's Fairy Tales*. He reviled Ibsen and defended Rostand (perhaps indefensibly), but the Trolls and the creator of *Peer Gynt* were the stuff his dreams were made of. That discord, that precarious subjection of a demoniacal will, defines Chesterton's nature."[19]

Marie Smith states,

> At the Slade, surrounded by juvenile manifestations of Decadence, he believed himself to be going mad and had to fight a tremendous battle to free himself of his own morbid thoughts, which were dominated by images of cruelty and

---

[18] Schmude, 100.

[19] Jorge Luis Borges, *Other Inquisitions, 1937-1952* (University of Texas Press: Austin, 2000), p. 84.

violence. That he succeeded is unremarkable; most adolescents do. But the manner in which he did it was strange, taking the form of a sort of willed optimism which expressed itself in a newfound delight in the world, literally, an awakening. Yet, even when he seemed to be writing in the highest spirits, horrors were never far away. It was something of which Chesterton himself was only too well aware.[20]

Dale Ahlquist comments on this view:

> I don't know. Anybody with a good imagination can imagine evil in unlikely and unwelcome manifestations. Who doesn't believe that the dark hides things that we don't want to know about? It doesn't mean that these fears are 'central.' I think we have to trust Chesterton when he says he will ride the nightmare and not let the nightmare ride him. It is a ride he takes only occasionally, and in any case, he is in control.[21]

However, Schmude points out that an observation similar to Borges's was made by Malcolm Muggeridge after he re-read Chesterton's autobiography in the 1960s:

> 'Underneath the happy Christian and happy husband, the lover of peasants, Fleet Street roistering and country inns, one senses in Chesterton a brooding, anguished, frightened spirit; a frustrated romantic, a displaced person, a letter delivered at the wrong address.' This view of Chesterton may indeed be an exaggeration. However, this insight into the darker depths of Chesterton's being do capture a key truth about him—one that can be readily documented and

---

[20] G.K. Chesterton, "Daylight and Nightmare," *Uncollected Stories and Fables* (Chivers Press, Bath, England, 1988), p. 6.

[21] Dale Ahlquist, "Lecture 89: Daylight and Nightmare," *Chesterton 101 Lecture Series*.http://www.chesterton.org/lecture-89/. 20 Jun. 2014.

should not be ignored, and that is certainly pertinent to any inquiry into his inner life.

Before I read this article Borges was only a name to me. But when I did some net surfing I was pleasantly surprised that he had had a deep appreciation of Chesterton. He considered Chesterton as one of his main inspirations, especially in his (Borges') own detective fiction. He translated some of the *Father Brown* stories into Spanish. And even though he said that "it was a pity that he [Chesterton] became a Catholic," and that he thought that in a couple hundred years Chesterton would "only be a figure in the histories of literature," he also said that he had a great affection for Chesterton. He said: "Literature is one of the forms that happiness takes; perhaps no writer has given me as many happy hours as Chesterton."[22] It is because of this love and appreciation of Chesterton that I can accept as particularly penetrating and possibly valid, his above comment about what he saw beneath the "surface sparkle" of Chesterton. It's an observation that comes out of love.

This same trait of Chesterton's is the central theme of Ralph Wood's recent book *Chesterton, the Nightmare Goodness of God*.[23] His quotes from Chesterton's autobiography seem to express more than an ordinary awareness of evil:

> I was still oppressed with the metaphysical nightmare of negations about mind and matter, with the morbid imagery of evil, with the burden of my own mysterious brain and body; but by this time I was in revolt against them; and trying to construct a healthier conception of cosmic life, even if it were one that should err on the side of health. I even called myself an optimist,

[22] Smith, p. 13.

[23] Ralph Wood, *Chesterton, the Nightmare Goodness of God* (Baylor University Press, 2011).

because I was so horribly near to being a pessimist.

When I had been for some time in these, the darkest depths of the contemporary pessimism, I had a strong inward impulse to revolt; to dislodge this incubus or throw off this nightmare.[24]

"To dislodge this incubus." Interestingly, when Wood quotes a definition of a nightmare it comes close to what Chesterton described he was fighting: "Originally referring to a witch or goblin, a nightmare was once understood as a female spirit or monster supposed to beset animals and people at night, settling on them when they are asleep, and producing a feeling of suffocation by its weight."[25]

Wood further comments: "I contend that there is another darker, more complex Chesterton, and that his daytime confidence about Christian things becomes fully persuasive only when examined in relation to his night-haunted terrors."[26] "The chief contention of this book is that Chesterton makes his deepest affirmations about God and man and the world in the face of nightmarish unbelief—the abiding fear that God's seemingly wondrous universe is, instead, devoid of divinity, that it is in fact a well-populated Hell unrecognized as such." "This book seeks, therefore, to reveal Chesterton's often nightmarish and Jacob-like encounter with the living One, so that we too might receive a blessing from this great fat jester of God whose work, like that of the angel at the River Jabbok, both wounds and blesses."[27]

These comments are all from Wood's Introduction, and thus it is his intention to speak of Chesterton's life and teaching as

---

[24] *Ibid.*, p. 2.

[25] *Ibid.*

[26] *Ibid.*, pp. 2-3.

[27] *Ibid.*, p. 6.

flowing, at least in part, from a "nightmarish unbelief." The "chief contention" of my present book is that an experience of the devil and a belief in devils is one aspect of Chesterton's "night-haunted terrors."

When I first read Wood's title I thought he was saying that Chesterton's understanding of God was colored, in some way, by a nightmarish attitude. He tries to make his theme explicit in his last chapter, which is entitled, "The Nightmare Mystery of Divine Action, *The Man Who Was Thursday*." It is not germane to my topic to go into his understanding of Chesterton's God except to say that since he concentrates exclusively on *Thursday* in that chapter, he is dealing with a very early understanding of Chesterton's God as when he (Wood) sees Sunday as an image of God. When Chesterton was asked whom he meant by Sunday, he said: "I think you can take him to stand for Nature as distinguished from God. Huge, boisterous, full of vitality, dancing with a hundred legs, bright with the glare of the sun, and at first sight somewhat regardless of us and our desires."[28]

Just as Chesterton said about nightmares that "I will ride on the Nightmare, but she shall not ride on me," so I don't find in his later writings any "nightmarish" muse "riding" Chesterton regarding his understanding of God. My book on him as a mystic attempted to demonstrate his extraordinary awareness of the goodness of God.

Wood quotes Chesterton's statement we saw above about the world being "nearly reasonable, but not quite." And in the early controversy with Blatchford (1903), he says this about the origin of religion: "Religion arose because there are incurable contradictions, impossible paradoxes in existence itself. There are vital riddles in life itself."

---

[28] G.K. Chesterton, *The Speaker*, "Leviathan and the Hook," (September 7, 1905). Quoted by Gary Wills, pp. 25-26.

These statements are keys to Chesterton's understanding of God. Like Job we are filled with questions about the why of existence, and thus we experience the world as a kind of riddle, just reasonable enough but not quite. We have to "figure it out." (Someone asked Bertrand Russell, the famous atheist, what he will say to God when he meets him. He said, "I will say, 'Sir, you know that the evidence for your existence was very inadequate.'") I like Gary Wills' description of Chesterton's God as "the riddling God" of Job. Chesterton said that the *Iliad* was a great book because life is a battle. And the *Odyssey* is a great book because life is a journey. And Job is a great book because life is a riddle. Job was probably Chesterton's favorite book of the Old Testament. And Job's God doesn't give answers, he just multiplies the questions: "Where were you when I laid the foundations of the earth?" In my book *The Tumbler of God*, Chapter Eleven is my understanding that Job is Chesterton's muse when he thinks about God.

I will not presume to try and psychoanalyze G.K. Chesterton! I will simply offer a "mystical" explanation to this dark side of Chesterton's experience as a complement to the mystical grace of wonder I sought to demonstrate in *The Tumbler of God*.

As mentioned above, in that book I sought to demonstrate that Chesterton had a mystical grace, which consisted in his profound awareness of a good God constantly bringing forth everything. This was the main source of his wonder and joy. A common criticism against Chesterton being a mystic of any kind is the oft-repeated opinion that he didn't suffer very much. It's often pointed out that real mystics have gone through terrible sufferings. Did Chesterton ever have a "dark night of the soul" *ala* St. John of the Cross? In *Tumbler* I offered a few responses to this objection. Basically I said that not all mystics suffer to the same extent; that one can receive a genuine mystical grace without a great deal of suffering; and I pointed out some of his ordinary human sufferings. But the insights of Borges and Muggeridge, and now Wood, have led me to a possibly deeper understanding of Chesterton's sufferings, and of his awareness of the reality of personal evil.

If Chesterton received, as I argue in *Tumbler*, a powerful mystical grace of being aware of God's on-going creativity, of a God "immortally active," could he not also have received, as a complement to this grace, *a mystical awareness of the depth of human depravity in himself and in the world*? Schmude quotes this comment by Chesterton from the *Autobiography*: "That the Catholic Church knew more about good than I did was easy to believe. That she knew more about evil than I did seemed incredible." This comment implies a more than ordinary experience and awareness of evil *within himself*. Besides Chesterton's encounter with evil spirits (which we shall explore), it's very possible that, along with his mystical grace of the experience of the ongoing creativity of the Creator, he was also given a mystical awareness of the reality of evil within himself.

Often mystics testify that before they received extraordinary graces they experienced a very profound and painful awareness of their sinfulness. This is a purification to prepare them for the beauties about to be revealed to them, and the graces they will receive. Perhaps these experiences of desolation are also given to the mystics to ground them in humility before the reception of more positive and exalted gifts of the Spirit. When Chesterton was asked what he thought about hell he replied that he had never been there himself, nor did he know anyone who had been there; but he understood it was a place to be avoided. But even if he hadn't been there, could he have been given a *taste* of hell?

In Chapter Six I will be briefly treating George MacDonald's possible influence on Chesterton. I came across a scene in one of MacDonald's fantasies that describes the above point I am trying to make here, namely, that before the reception of grace, purification is often the prelude. Many such examples could be given from the lives of the saints.

Rolland Hein is a MacDonald scholar. In his book *Harmony Within: the Spiritual Vision of George MacDonald*, he gives an interpretation of a scene from *The Princess and Curdie*. Curdie is with the Grandmother (God) in the presence of a fire "glowing, flaming roses, red and white." He is being prepared for a demanding task. He is commanded to thrust his hands into the fire. When the pain subsides he withdraws his hands to find that they have become white, smooth, and tender. The Queen tells him that he has received a supernatural gift. Here is Hein's interpretation:

> MacDonald is building this scene upon principles very important in his theology. The fire of roses suggests that those destined by God to perform a particular task must first be spiritually prepared. They are truly 'elect,' a term MacDonald understands to designate those who are selected to service, rather than designating in a Calvinist sense those who are selected for salvation from hell. This service requires preparation. God makes his servants fit for His work by purging them of what in their lives may displease Him.[29]

I think it is very probable that, along with an experiential grace of the goodness of all things, Chesterton was also given some sort of grace of experiencing the depth of evil in the "fire of roses." We all have had some minimal realization of this kind of pain. But the insight of Borges may well be true, and I would understand it in this mystical sense: it was not essentially due

---

[29] Rolland Hein, *The Harmony Within: The Spiritual Vision of George MacDonald* (Sunrise Book Publishers: Eureka, California, 1989), p. 40.

to anything psychological or to the decadent culture around him, *but to a special grace.*

And could not one dimension of this experience of the depth of evil in himself and in the world be also an experience of the awesomeness of God, not to say the frightful reality of God? This is at the heart of Wood's book: "To speak of God's goodness as nightmarish is not to indulge in wanton and idle use of paradox. On the contrary, it is an effort to overcome the mistake of reading the grace and mercy of God as something always cheering and comforting."[30] This is also what he is implying when he speaks of a Jacob-like encounter with the living One.

After all, there are enough experiences of God in the scriptures that attest to the Holy One as *terribilis et tremendum*. Wood also indicates this as an aspect of Chesterton's "Nightmarish" experience of God: "Rudolf Otto taught us long ago that the numinous must always be understood as the *mysterium tremendum et fascinans*, the Sacred that alarms at the same time it allures. This is the lesson that Job learns in the whirlwind of the divine epiphany and that the author of Hebrews confirms: 'It is a fearful thing to fall into the hands of the living God.' (Heb. 10:31) Chesterton thus depicts this silent and invisible Presence as no less frightening than enticing, especially in its twilight manifestations, when evening slips into darkness."[31]

Chesterton could have received a special mystical grace that was the reverse of the depth of his experience of the goodness of the immortally active God—*a grace about his own sinfulness and the terribilis of God.*

Schmude quotes from a letter to Msgr. Ronald Knox, which I found to be an extraordinary and rare sharing by Chesterton

---

[30] Wood, p. 6.

[31] Wood, p. 115. Cf. Rudolf Otto, *The Idea of the Holy* (Martino Fine Books, 2010).

of his inner life. He was really a very private person about his interior world. This quote gives an insight into the depths of his "brooding on doubts and dirt and daydreams" and his "morbid life of the lonely mind":

> I am in a state now when I feel a monstrous charlatan, as if I wore a mask and were muffled with cushions, whenever I see anything about the public G.K.C. It hurts me, for though the views I express are real, the image is horribly unreal compared with the real person who needs help just now. I have as much vanity as anybody about any of these superficial successes while they are going on; *but I never feel for a moment that they affect the reality of whether I am utterly rotten or not* [emphasis mine]; so that any public comments on my religious position seem like a wind on the other side of the world; as if they were about somebody else—as indeed they are. I am not troubled about a great fat man who appears on platforms and in caricatures; even when he enjoys controversies on what I believe to be the right side. I am concerned about what has become of a little boy whose father showed him a toy theatre, and a schoolboy whom nobody ever heard of, with his brooding on doubts and dirt and daydreams, of crude conscientiousness so inconsistent as to be near a hypocrisy; and all the morbid life of the lonely mind of a living person with whom I have lived. It is that story that so often came near to ending badly, that I want to end well.

"Whether I am utterly rotten or not. The morbid life of the lonely mind." Who would have ever dared to attribute such states to Chesterton! And yet, he attributes them to himself.

When Father Brown shows his penetrating insights into a crime, the suspect asks: "Are you a devil?" "I am a man," answered

Father Brown, "and therefore have all the devils in my heart."[32] Chesterton had some acute awareness of the devils within his own heart. "The sane man knows that he has a touch of the beast, a touch of the devil, a touch of the saint, a touch of the citizen. The really sane man knows that he has the touch of the madman."[33]

Chesterton said once that the story that became the most fundamental inspiration in his life was George MacDonald's *The Princess and the Goblins*.[34] Besides the wonderful great fairy grandmother in the attic, and "the magic thread as a symbol for the contradictory nature of religious discernment,"[35] there were the goblins below. In Chapter Six I inquire more deeply into who the goblins might represent.

One of the main themes in Chesterton's thought is that belief in the devil helps to clarify where the battle lines are. The depths of his own interior loneliness, brooding, and darkness was another foil that made the goodness in himself and in creation shine more brightly.

When treating of this theme in Chesterton's character, reference is invariably made to his essay "The Diabolist." The author of the second article, George Bull, refers to this essay, as does Knight. I will quote a few lines from his article to show that others also see this aspect of Chesterton as very important to an understanding of his vision of life:

> Chesterton's spirituality, however, had more to it than the serenity and good humor of a naturally happy disposition. The crucial decision of his spiritual life was taken in his teens when he realised he was experiencing sighting of, and a fascination

---

[32] *The Complete Father Brown*, p. 87.

[33] *Ibid.*

[34] *G.K.C. As M.C.*, pp. 164-165.

[35] Oddie, p. 36.

with, a starkly evil phenomenon.

The almost obsessive concern with the nature of evil, the existence of the devil, and the sinfulness of mankind which he was wretchedly sure he shared, are continuing threads in Chesterton's creative life. Another of his perceptive biographers, Dudley Barker, observes that the reality and lure of evil, powerful and personal, is portrayed in one way or another in most of his books.

The roots of Chesterton's spirituality are in his early grasp of his own propensity to evil which intensified the exuberance of his delight in the actuality, beauty and beneficence of God's creation.

THE RED ANGEL

Another additional explanation to Chesterton's "brooding on doubts and dirt and daydreams," occurs in his essay "The Red Angel." A woman writes to him that it is cruel to tell children fairy tales because it frightens them. His basic response is that frightening things are in the child prior to the fairy tales. "If you keep bogies and goblins away from children they would make them up for themselves":

> One small child in the dark can invent more hells than Swendenborg. One small child can imagine monsters too big and black to get into any picture, and give them names too unearthly and cacophonous to have occurred in the cries of any lunatic. The child, to begin with, commonly likes horrors, and he continues to indulge in them even when he does not like them. The fear does not come from fairy tales; the fear comes from the universe of the soul. Fairy tales do not give the child the idea of the evil or the ugly; that is in the children

already, because it is in the world already.[36]

We do not have to get into a discussion of whether this is true or not. (Think of your own experience; it certainly corresponds with mine: I was afraid of who or what was in the dark of our cellar long before I read any fairy tales.) In any case, Chesterton certainly believed this was part of his experience. And if we all agree that he was an exceptionally sensitive child, could not this "fear that comes from the universe of the soul" be an additional cause for the "morbid life of his lonely mind," and an experience common to us all?

And more pertinent to my topic:

> Take the most horrible of Grimm's tales in incident and imagery, the excellent tale of the 'Boy Who Could not Shudder,' and you will see what I mean. There are some shocks in that tale. I remember especially a man's legs which fell down from the chimney by themselves and walked about the room, until they were rejoined by the severed head and body which fell down the chimney after them. That is very good. But the point of the story and the point of the reader's feelings is not that these things are frightening, but the far more striking fact that the hero was not frightened at them. The most fearful of all these fearful wonders was his own absence of fear. He slapped the bogies on the back and asked the devils to drink wine with him; many a time in my youth, when stifled with some modern morbidity, I have prayed for a double portion of his spirit. If you have not read the end of his story, go and read it; it is the wisest thing in the world.

I did go and read it. My translation read "The Youth who

---

[36] "The Red Angel" in *Tremendous Trifles* (Sheed & Ward: New York, 1955), pp. 85-89. The remaining quotes are from this essay.

could not Shiver and Shake." To help him overcome his lack of fear someone dresses up as a ghost at night to scare him; he is told to camp out at night in the presence of several criminals hanging from a tree. These are all human attempts to get him to shiver and shake. But the last one borders more on the diabolical.

There is an enchanted castle where no one has survived three nights because of the terrors they encounter. The King has promised that whoever can survive this trial can have his beautiful daughter in marriage. Our hero is all for it.

The human race has a general, common experience of diabolical manifestations: black ferocious animals—like mad dogs; dismembered humans holding skulls in their hands; corpses rising out of coffins. Our intrepid youth encounters many of these in the castle nights, but, of course, is not afraid of them. It is of these last that Chesterton had in mind when he asked for a "double portion of his spirit" in his own fears. (The phrase, of course, comes from 2 Kings (2:9) when Elisha asks Elias, before his departure, "Let me inherit a double portion of your spirit.") In the face of especially diabolical attacks, Chesterton asked for a double portion of the lad without fear.

The growth of this spirit within Chesterton was expressed in some of his poems, for example, "The Kingdom of Heaven." We shall see the entire poem later, but this stanza is relevant for now:

> Said the Lord God, 'Build a house,
> Build it in the gorge of death,
> Found it in the throats of hell.
> Where the lost sea muttereth,
> Fires and whirlwinds, build it well.'

He prayed, during his life, to face the demons, and used the muse of the "Youth who could not Shudder" as one of his inspirations.

As well, some of Chesterton's battling spirit comes from what he learned from fairy tales that give the child his first clear idea of the possible *defeat of bogey*. The baby has known the dragon intimately ever since he had an imagination. "What the fairy tales provides for him is a St. George to kill the dragon. Exactly what the fairy tale does is this: it accustoms him for a series of clear pictures to the idea that these limitless terrors had a limit, that there is something in the universe more mystical than darkness, and stronger than strong fear."

> At the four corners of a child's bed stand Perseus and Roland, Sigurd and St. George. If you withdraw the guard of heroes you are not making him rational; you are only leaving him to fight the devils alone. For the devils, alas, we have always believed in. The gloomy view of the universe has been a continuous tradition; and the new types of spiritual investigation or conjecture all begin by being gloomy. A little while ago men believed in no spirits. Now they are beginning rather slowly to believe in rather slow spirits.

Are not all detective stories morality plays? The good guys always win, and the bad guys are caught and punished. In the Father Brown stories it is St. George in a clerical suit and collar battling the demons in the darkness of the mind; and proving by his excellent detective work that the "limitless terrors" of human criminality "have a limit"?

CHAPTER TWO

"The Devil Made Me Do It"
CHESTERTON PUTS ON HIS ARMOR

The second more obvious origin of Chesterton's awareness of evil is his actual encounter with the devil. The contention of this book is that belief in the devil was one of the primary factors that made Chesterton into a battling warrior for the Good, the True, and the Beautiful—for God.

The devil is stupid as well as devious. (We will see in Chapter Six that George MacDonald thought the temptations in the wilderness were really *silly* diabolical attempts to present to the Lord!) When Chesterton was dabbling in the murkier regions of the human soul, the devil thought he would finally win him to his side by making himself known in a very tangible way. It backfired. Chesterton's encounter with the Evil One was one of the most powerful of all the knocks on his head from reality he ever received. His heart was too big to be satisfied with evil and nothingness as the ultimate explanation of everything. He reasoned that if there were evil forces there must be something "more mystical than darkness, and stronger than strong fear." And he dedicated his life to fighting for the uproarious life and joy at the heart of all things.

In this chapter I want to show how Chesterton first encountered the devil; and then how pervasive, in his writings and thinking, was belief in the demons. But before coming to that I want to expand on the previously mentioned theory, namely, that sometimes Chesterton is seen as not taking the evil in the world too seriously. And then I wish to answer some other objections to his character that will lend added weight to his battle with evil.

A criticism by Henry Murray that appeared in the *Bookman* in 1910 well expresses a common opinion of Chesterton:

> The real paradox about Mr. Chesterton…is that, with a tender and overflowing affection for all sentient things, he seems almost completely ignorant of the existence of sorrow or suffering…He has amused and tickled thousands…but I cannot imagine that he has ever given one solitary individual a moist eye or a lump in the throat. Pathos and tragedy are notes, or rather entire octaves, lacking from his keyboard. His boisterous optimism will not admit that there is anything to sorrow over in this best of all possible worlds.[1]

Surprisingly, Belloc also seemed to lean in this direction. He thought that Chesterton didn't wound his opponents sufficiently: "You do not rise from the reading of one of Chesterton's appreciations with that feeling of being armed which you obtain from the great satirists and particularly from the masters of irony. He wounded none, but thus also he failed to provide weapons wherewith one may wound and kill folly. Now without wounding and killing, there is no battle; and thus, in this life, no victory; but also no peril to the soul through hatred."[2] Joseph Pearce comments: "It does not follow that one must wound people in order to provide weapons to wound and kill folly."[3]

Wood comments and quotes Chesterton who, as usual, has the best insights into his convictions:

---

[1] Knight, p. 17, Quoting Conlon, *Critical Judgments*, pp. 237-38.

[2] Pearce, p. 60.

[3] *Ibid.*

In a world becoming immune to the Gospel, Chesterton believed that only those art forms that have the disruptive power of mime and even melodrama can capture the Gospel's joyful outrageousness, its fantastic eccentricity, its scandalously glad claim that God himself has entered this human fray in Israel and Christ and the Church. 'Of all the varied forms of the literature of joy,' Chesterton claimed, 'the form most truly worthy of moral reverence and artistic ambition is the form called "farce"—or its wilder shape in pantomime.'[4]

And in a footnote to the above passage, Wood has this: "Chesterton makes the surprising claim that, while 'black and catastrophic' pain attracts the immature artist, 'joy is a far more elusive and elfish matter, since it is our reason for existing, and a very feminine reason; it mingles with every breath we draw and every cup of tea we drink.' Precisely because joy remains largely unrecognized in its invisible ubiquity, it requires extraordinary modes of expression."[5]

Are not many tempted to think sometimes that Chesterton is certainly a profound thinker but he just doesn't make it to the heights—or depths—of truth, holiness, or what life is really all about? Why? Well, he's just too playful, too whimsical and, yes, too funny to be seen as any kind of guide to ultimate things. Does he really take life seriously? Is he aware of the evil in the world, and does he come to terms with it? Even in his novel *The Ball and the Cross*, even here, when discussing (in my view) the cataclysmic and apocalyptic matters of the Antichrist and the end of the world, he insists on treating them in his fantastical and fanciful ways!

---

[4] Wood, p. 133.

[5] *Ibid.*, p. 297. Chesterton quotes are from, "A Defense of Farce," in *The Defendant*, pp. 124-125. Cf. also Wood's book, *The Comedy of Redemption*, Christian Faith and Comic Vision in Four American Novelists. It is a profound argument that comedy is deeper than tragedy.

After all, isn't life ultimately very serious? I mean, there is the Lord on the cross, and Buddha not exactly laughing about life (although he does, at times, seem to have an enigmatic smile). And then there are all the very serious desert mothers and fathers and the writings of the saints on the spiritual life, and the Last Judgment, and Hell and, well, you know, isn't it ultimately all very solemn, grave and somber? And where is his "tragic sense of life" which is supposed to be one of the essential ingredients of human existence?

Perhaps—the criticisms continue—Chesterton's attitude and style are due to the fact that he didn't really suffer all that much compared with other greats and with most mystics. The following account in his *Autobiography* of his suffering as a youngster is not exactly that of an abused child! He is serious here: "I was by no means unacquainted with pain, which is a pretty unanswerable thing: I had a fair amount of toothache and especially earache; and few can bemuse themselves into regarding earache as a form of epicurean hedonism."[6]

The Greeks used to say that you couldn't learn anything worthwhile without suffering; and Dostoyevsky said there are some truths about human existence that we will never know without pain. Was Chesterton's vision of life born out of any real affliction beyond that of normal mortals? Did he elude the effort of blood and tears and regain paradise through the power of positive thinking?

I will argue in this book that precisely *because* he arrived at such profound truths *he must have suffered*. If you arrive at truth about life you must have gone through some pain and distress to get there. Besides the possible "mystical" experience

---

[6] G.K. Chesterton, *Autobiography* (Ignatius Press: San Francisco, 2006).

of evil I mentioned above, and besides the normal human sufferings, Chesterton suffered intensely *on the battlefields of the mind.*

A Gnostic?

A thought is a deed, an act; thinking is also action. We tend to assume that action only concerns bodily movement, and thinking is, well, is not action—it's just thinking. But serious thinking is work, and for Chesterton it was his primary battleground. Constantly challenging falsehoods wherever you discover them is really work, real conflict, and real battle. The conflict of ideas affects your personal relationships, especially if you're such a public person as Chesterton was. It affects your health as well.

And the enormity of his output! Did he not perhaps work himself to death by battling too long and too indefatigably on the ramparts of the mind? He arrived at his celebrated positive view of life not from the power of "positive thinking" but from, among other things, his battle with evil.

But was Chesterton a Gnostic, someone conjuring up theories of reality out of his enormously creative imagination? St. Anthony lived in a pagan world; and Gnostic systems were rampant in the civilized pockets of that world.[7] At the turn of the 19th century, was Chesterton affected by the temptation to invent his own system of reality?

The criticism that Chesterton's approach to reality is rather Gnostic and dreamlike, lacking the pain, sorrow, and the battle with evil which alone gives one the right to speak about the hidden glory of creation, is not new. Listen to a very early criticism of Chesterton that many people continue to apply to his vast intellectual output. It is C.F.G. Masterman's review of

---

[7] Cf. St. Irenaeus, *Against All Heresies.*

Chesterton's book, *The Defendant*. He entitled his review "The Blasphemy of Optimism":

> Mr. Chesterton holds that all things are very good. He may assert that he has a certain reputable precedent for such a statement. The plea cannot be entertained. God found all things 'very good.' Such a discovery is a prerogative of divinity. No man can look on God and live; and no man can live who sees things as God sees them. Optimism in men is an indication of death. Genial acquiescence in intolerable things is the great conservative force of the world.
>
> Mr. Chesterton, in effect, is attempting a short cut to Paradise. He would fain elude the effort of blood and tears by which alone that Paradise can be regained. That the world is full of glories to those who have eyes to see is a commonplace appealing to each generation as a grotesque and startling novelty. But the seeing eye is not attained by the manufacture of a joyful noise in the dark.[8]

I like the criticism that "no man can live who sees things as God sees them." Of course, Chesterton did not have God's full vision of things, but with his mystical grace he had more of it than most of us! This was the source of his exuberance and joy.

I believe our critic here is calling Chesterton a Gnostic, although the word isn't used. "Gnostic" is a bad word now in the Christian tradition, although if you go back far enough, Clement of Alexandria called Christians the true gnostics because in Christ they really knew what reality was all about. False gnostics concoct imaginary worlds unrelated to scripture, tradition, or sound philosophical thinking. Chesterton was never accused of this extreme form of Gnosticism, but an element of gnostic

---

[8] Quoted by D.J. Conlon, in *G.K. Chesterton, The Critical Judgments*, pp. 40-45.

thought—implied by Masterman—is that you can achieve reality merely by thinking about it. You can "get there" just by changing your mind. This was the essence of Masterman's criticism.

Thus, Chesterton "manufactures" reality also. He just thinks beautiful thoughts and presto! He is back in paradise. "The man with the muck rake," Chesterton would say, "can obtain the golden crown, not by the painful effort to look upwards, but by weaving the sticks on the floor into a coronet and assuring himself that it is gold."[9] Chesterton's world may be true, but he gets there too easily. Thus, he is accused of attaining such a vision without a fight:

> Persistent effort, the sweat and blood of men, wreckage of a thousand lives and a world travail of pain, has been the price men have paid for permission sometimes to whisper to each other in the darkness that all things are very good. The greatest tragedy in history, at which the sun veiled his face and the pillars of the earth were shaken, was necessary to enable humanity to cherish for nineteen centuries the desperate hope that God is Love.[10]

To support Masterman's criticism it would be possible to muster a number of statements from Chesterton that *seem* to confirm such Gnosticism. One of my all-time favorites that could be so misunderstood is the following:

> Religion has had to provide that longest and strangest telescope—the telescope through which we could see the star upon which we dwelt. For the mind and eyes of the average man and this world is as lost as Eden and as sunken as Atlantis. There runs a strange law through the length of human history—that

---

[9] *Ibid.*, p. 44.
[10] *Ibid.*, p. 45.

men are continually tending to undervalue their environment, to undervalue their happiness, to undervalue themselves. The great sin of mankind, the sin typified by the fall of Adam, is the tendency, not towards pride, but towards this weird and horrible humility. This is the great fall, the fall by which the fish forgets the sea, the ox forgets the meadow, the clerk forgets the city, everyman forgets his environment, and, in the fullest and most literal sense, forgets himself. Most probably we are in Eden still. It is only our eyes that have changed.[11]

"It is only our eyes that have changed." So, all we have to do is refocus our eyes and we will have the perfect vision of reality, right? Yes and no. "Yes," if you understood by "eyes" what Chesterton meant, the eyes of faith. No, if you think such a vision can be obtained without effort or pain or the search for truth.

Chesterton was well aware of the perils of Gnosticism, and that only *dogma* could protect us:

> Nothing else than dogma could have resisted the riot of imaginative invention with which the [Gnostics] were waging their war on nature; with their Aeons and Demiurge, their strange Logos and their sinister Sophia. If the Church had not insisted on theology, it would have melted into a mad mythology of the mystics, yet further removed from reason and even from rationalism; and, above all, yet further removed from life and from the love of life.[12]

It is the whole thrust of our mystical and ascetical tradition that a deeply Christian vision of life—the eyes of faith—is not acquired cheaply. (Bonhoeffer called it "cheap grace.") To change

---

[11] G.K. Chesterton, *The Defendant* (Dover Publications: New York, 2012), p. 3.

[12] *The Everlasting Man*, p. 229.

our eyes requires a change of heart. It's one of the essential points of this book to show that Chesterton believed in the necessity of this change of heart, and that he achieved his new eyes partly through the battle with evil. I shall try to show that Chesterton's vision was not born by simply making a joyful noise in the dark, but because he also heard noises from the Prince of Darkness, and fought against those insidious suggestions.

"The Sound of Battle"

As we continue our reflections on Chesterton's combat with evil, let us distinguish two levels in his life, the theoretical and the practical.

Did Chesterton think that his vision of the goodness of all things was attainable without a fight? Anyone who knows anything at all about him would consider such a view incomprehensible. Even as early as his review in 1902, Masterman would have had several volumes of Chesterton's poetry to examine. Charles Williams, a great literary artist himself, says that the basic theme of all Chesterton's poetry is "the sound of battle":

> Mr. Chesterton's verse, even when it is not concerned with historic battles—Ethandune, Lepanto, the Marne—has generally the sound of a battle within it. There are drawn swords from the first page to the last: material, intellectual and spiritual; the swords of Arthur and Roland, of the Mother of God and Michael the Archangel. Everything is spoken of in terms of war, either actual or potential. For even when there is no enemy, the state of being described [by Chesterton] is a state where man is strung to a high pitch of expectation and his delight is already militant. The babe unborn in one poem looks forward to 'leave to weep and fight', and his old men die

either in conflict or in the joy or fear of conflict. Man must be either a hero or a coward.[13]

This is certainly one of Chesterton's fundamental views of reality:

> To the Orthodox there must always be a case for revolution; for in the hearts of men God has been put under the feet of Satan. In the upper world hell once rebelled against heaven. But in this world heaven is rebelling against hell. For the orthodox there can always be a revolution, for a revolution is a restoration. At any instant you may strike a blow for the perfection of which no man has seen since Adam. This world can be made beautiful again by beholding it as a battlefield. When we have defined and isolated the evil thing, the colours come back into everything else.[14]

And who but Chesterton could describe a Gothic Cathedral in the following terms:

> The truth about Gothic is, first, that it is alive, and second, that it is on the march. It is the Church Militant. All its spires are spears at rest; and all its stones are stones asleep in a catapult. In that instant of illusion, I could hear the arches clash like swords as they crossed each other. The mighty and numberless columns seemed to go swinging by like the huge feet of imperial elephants. The graven foliage wreathed and blew like banners going into battle; the silence was deafening with all the mingled noises of a military march; the great

---

[13] *The Collected Works of G.K. Chesterton*, Vol. X Collected Poetry, Part I (Ignatius Press: San Francisco, 1983), "General Editor's Introduction," p. 8. Cf. Wood, Chapter 3, "Militarism and the Church Militant," for a treatment of Chesterton's thinking on war and pacifism, pp. 69-96.

[14] G.K. Chesterton, *Orthodoxy* (Ignatius Press: San Francisco, 1995), p. 117.

bell shook down, as the organ shook up its thunder. The thirsty-throated gargoyles shouted like trumpets from all the roofs and pinnacles as they passed; and from the lectern in the core of the cathedral the eagle of the awful evangelist clashed his wings of brass.[15]

This theme of battle was also part of his motivation for becoming a Catholic. In a letter to his mother he wrote: "I think as Cecil did, that the fight for the family and the free citizen and everything decent must now be waged by the one fighting form of Christianity."[16] And in the *Toronto Daily Star*: "I have no use for a Church which is not a Church militant, which cannot order battle and fall in line and march in the same direction."[17]

Masterman thought Chesterton imaginatively turned bad things into good, disregarding the obvious evils of the world. But Chesterton knew the insisted on real evil, especially in the face of unreflective optimism that would dismiss or over look it.

If optimism means a general approval, it is certainly true that

---

[15] Quoted by Pearce, p. 178, from *Daily News*, 13 May, 1911. In a talk on the feast of Mary Magdalene when he was Pope, Benedict XVI referred to the war with Satan: "Among the 'lost sheep' whom Jesus saved there was a woman by the name Mary from the village of Magdala on the Sea of Galilee, for which reason she is known as Mary Magdalene. Her feast day falls today. Luke the Evangelist tells us that Jesus freed her from seven demons; in other words, He saved her from utter servitude to the Evil One. And, in what does this profound healing that God achieves through Jesus consist? It consists in true and complete peace, which is the result of the reconciliation of people in themselves and in all their relations: with God, with others and with the world. The Evil One always seeks to destroy the work of God by sowing strife in the human heart, between body and soul, between man and God, in interpersonal, social and international relations, even between man and the creation. The Evil One spreads war; God creates peace." Vatican Information Service, 23 Jul. 2012.

[16] Maisie Ward, *Gilbert Keith Chesterton*, p. 396. Quoted by Pearce, p. 269.

[17] O'Connor, *Father Brown on Chesterton,* pp. 139-41. Quoted by Pearce, p. 279.

the more a man becomes an optimist the more he becomes a melancholy man. If he manages to praise everything, his praise will develop an alarming resemblance to a polite boredom. He will say that the marsh is as good as the garden; he will mean that the garden is as dull as the marsh. He may force himself to say that emptiness is good, but he will hardly prevent himself from asking what is the good of such good. This optimism does exist - this optimism which is more hopeless than pessimism - this optimism which is the very heart of hell. Against such an aching vacuum of joyless approval there is only one antidote - a sudden and pugnacious belief in positive evil. This world can be made beautiful again by beholding it as a battlefield. When we have defined and isolated the evil thing, the colours come back into everything else. When evil things have become evil, good things, in a blazing apocalypse, become good. There are some men who are dreary because they do not believe in God; but there are many others who are dreary because they do not believe in the devil. The grass grows green again when we believe in the devil, the roses grow red again when we believe in the devil… [T]he true optimist can only continue an optimist so long as he is discontented. For the full value of this life can only be got by fighting; the violent take it by storm. And if we have accepted everything, we have missed something - war. This life of ours is a very enjoyable fight, but a very miserable truce.[18]

---

[18] G.K. Chesterton, *The Collected Works of G.K. Chesterton*, Vol. 15 (Ignatius Press: San Francisco), pp. 201-202.

Hymn for the Church Militant

A "Hymn for the Church Militant"[19] is surely one of Chesterton's "noblest works." It expresses the attitudes with which a Christian should fight. Christians could meditate on it at least once a week to avoid any triumphalism in their holy war for the faith. The devil hates humility. The petitions expressed in this poem, if devotedly prayed for, would help to defeat the devil's strategy of causing division. Chesterton knew how to fight while making friends of his opponents.

> Great God, that bowest sky and star,
> Bow down our towering thoughts to thee,
> And grant us in a faltering war,
> The firm feet of humility.
> Lord, we that snatch the swords of flame,
> Lord, we that cry about Thy car,
> We, too are weak with pride and shame,
> We too are as our foemen are.
> Yes, we are mad as they are mad,
> Yea, we are blind as they are blind,
> Yea, we are very sick and sad
> Who bring good news to all mankind.
> The dreadful joy Thy Son has sent,
> Is heavier than any care.
> We find, as Cain his punishment,
> Our pardon more than we can bear.
> Lord, when we cry Thee far and near
> And thunder through all lands unknown,
> The gospel into every ear,
> Lord, let us not forget our own.

---

[19] Comment by Wood, p. 63, who quotes the poem from *Collected Poetry, Part 1*, pp. 141-42.

Cleanse us from ire of creed or class,
The anger of the idle kings;
Sow in our souls, like living grass,
The laughter of all lowly things.

It is a sign of the genius of Chesterton that people can find contradictory views in his writings, as in the two opposite views above. That's because his thinking covers so very many aspects of life that anyone—friend or foe—can find something to their liking. If you're a pessimist or optimist, a pacifist or a warrior, a Catholic or a Protestant, an artist or a Philistine, a believer or unbeliever in Christ, pro-Jewish or anti-Jewish, a patriot of your country or a traitor, and on and on—whatever—you could probably find something in Chesterton that would provide you material for an essay. That's because he touched on all aspects of life. (Belloc said that the Catholic Church suffers so much persecution because it has strong teachings on every aspect of life.)

Many people do not often see the point Chesterton is making; many don't take him seriously; many are selective. In reading criticisms of Chesterton's views over the years one will come across pros and cons about every conceivable opinion. He could often see a kernel of truth in every opinion even if he did not entirely agree with it. (Emeritus Pope Benedict said that there is some truth in every heresy.) People often took this kernel of truth that Chesterton acknowledged as agreement, or they sometimes took it out of context. The multiplicity of his statements on every conceivable topic was a sign of the great breadth of his mind, his *complete* mind.

THE CHURCH ON THE OFFENSIVE

I remember reading years ago in C.S. Lewis that the Church is involved in a "mopping up operation." This is not a very glorious description for the new evangelization! After the resurrection the victory has been won, Hades has been emptied, and the demons know that the main citadel has been taken. But, as in a battle when the capitol has been taken, there are often forces out in the hills somewhere who haven't heard that the war is over—or refuse to accept that it *is* over. (A pertinent twenty-first century example was the holdout of Gaddafi loyalists in his hometown. All communication had been cut off, so many did not know that Tripoli had been taken.)

It's the Church's mission to go into the whole world and tell everyone that the battle is over. The demons, who know that Christ has won the victory, keep trying to convince everyone—by lying, or by keeping the truth from them—that the battle is *not* over, that Christ is *not* God, that he has *not* risen from the dead, that you are *still in your sins*, and blah, blah, blah. The Holy Spirit, the *Parakletos* (defense lawyer in Greek) testifies that Christ has won the victory.

"And so I say to you, you are Peter, and upon this rock I will build my church, and the gates of hell will not prevail against it."[20] Too often Christians understand this text as the Church being under siege, enclosed in a fortress surrounded by hostile forces as in Mansoul. On the contrary, the analogy is just the opposite: *it is the gates of hell that are being attacked.* In other words, the Church is *on the offensive.*

Chesterton was not afraid of the demons or of the terrors of hell. Indeed, he had received that double portion of the "youth who could not shiver or shake." In his poem "The Kingdom of Heaven" he has the Lord God commanding to build the house—the kingdom—in the "throats of hell," and to strive "with formless might and mirth" against the powers of hell. It is

---

[20] Matthew 16:18.

an obvious offensive attack, flaunting and deriding the powers of the netherworld:

> Said the Lord God, 'Build a house,
> Build it in the gorge of death,
> Found it in the throats of hell.
> Where the lost sea muttereth,
> Fires and whirlwinds, build it well.'
>
> Laboured sternly flame and wind.
> But a little, and they cry,
> 'Lord, we doubt of this Thy will.
> We are blind and murmur why,'
> And the winds are murmuring still.
>
> Said the Lord God, 'Build a house,
> Cleave its treasure from the earth,
> With the jarring powers of hell
> Strive with formless might and mirth,
> Tribes and war-men, build it well.'
>
> Then the raw red sons of men
> Brake the soil, and lopped the wood,
> But a little and they shrill,
> 'Lord, we cannot view Thy good,'
> And the wild men clamour still.
>
> Said the Lord God, 'Build a house,
> Smoke and iron, spark and steam,
> Speak and vote and buy and sell;
> Let a new world throb and stream,
> Seers and makers, build it well.'

Strove the cunning men and strong,
But a little and they cry,
'Lord, mayhap we are but clay,
And we cannot know the why,'
And the wise men doubt to-day.

Yet though worn and deaf and blind,
Force and savage, king and seer
Labour still, they know not why;
At the dim foundation here,
Knead and plough and think and ply.

Till at last, mayhap, hereon,
Fused of passion and accord,
Love its crown and peace its stay
Rise the city of the Lord
That we darkly build to-day.[21]

The line "Strive with formless might and mirth," reminds me of a remark by St. Teresa of Avila:

> If this Lord is powerful, as I see that He is and I know that He is, and if the devils are His slaves, what evil can they do to me since I am a servant of this Lord and King? Why shouldn't I have the fortitude to engage in combat with all of hell? There was no doubt, in my opinion, that they were afraid of me, for I remained so calm and so unafraid of them all. All the fears I usually felt left me—even to this day.[22]

And there were some tough desert mothers as well: "A certain

---

[21] *The Collected Poems of G.K. Chesterton* (London, 1971).

[22] Quoted in Gabriel Amorth, *An Exorcist Tells His Story* (Ignatius Press: San Francisco, 1999), p. 64.

Susan was once visited by a blessed and god-fearing monk. Each observed the other in combat with demons. Susan, however, proved stronger and more resilient. Not only did she get the best of the demons, she had no fear of them. She was unmovable, and the demons cried out: 'This is a woman, but she is stone, and instead of flesh she is iron.'"[23]

---

[23] Wilken, p. 105.

CHAPTER THREE

"I Am Not Proud of Knowing the Devil"
THE ENCOUNTER

The most powerful origin of Chesterton's belief in the father of lies is his actual encounter with a "lie telling" phenomenon.

In a section in his *Autobiography* he recounts his early dabbling with evil. Maisie Ward says of this period (he was almost nineteen): "Surrounded by pleasant friendships and home influences he had never really become aware of evil. Now it broke upon him suddenly."[1] His friends asked one another: "Is Chesterton going mad?"[2] This evil was not only the Evil One, but he was also going through an "extreme skepticism. As he expressed it, he 'felt as if everything might be a dream,' as if he had 'projected the universe from within [read "solipsism"].' The agnostic doubts the existence of God. Gilbert at moments doubted the existence of the agnostic."[3] He said that the spiritual significance of Impressionism in art contributed to this mental state:

> Whatever may be the merits of this method of art, there is obviously something highly subjective and skeptical about it as a method of thought. It naturally lends itself to the metaphysical suggestion that things only exist as we perceive them, or that things do not exist at all. The philosophy of Impressionism is necessarily close to the philosophy of illusion.

---

[1] Maisie Ward, *Gilbert Keith Chesterton*, p. 43.

[2] *Ibid.*, p. 44.

[3] *Ibid.*

I felt as if everything might be a dream. It was as if I had myself projected the universe from within, with its trees and stars; and that is so near to the notion of being God that it is manifestly even nearer to going mad.[4]

In other words, Chesterton was in a state of mental terror, uncertain as to whether he was or was not a *real* Gnostic. Not only was he afraid of making up reality in his mind, he was wondering if those ideas were all that existed. And it is significant that, in his *Autobiography*, before he relates the "rudimentary and makeshift mystical theory of his own" which helped him escape from pure subjectivism, he mentions the devil. A large part of his chapter, "How to be a Lunatic," is taken up with his experiences in spiritualism. Is he not saying, by this emphasis, that his experience of evil was also a factor in freeing him from this illusion?

My contention is that his experience of evil was one of the very significant factors that knocked him into reality, just as bumping his head against a wooden post plunged him into the heart of his own mysticism.

Early Encounter

The devil, as it were, over-played his hand: he knocked Chesterton over the head and exposed his satanic reality. By "introducing himself" to Chesterton he also plunged our hero into the existence of supernatural realities, and thus also into the world outside the mind. (One of the "side-benefits" of exorcism is that it increases one's faith in the truths of the Creed: when the devil becomes more real, so does the whole supernatural world.) The devil is stupid as well as sinister, and often is not aware of the "beneficial side-effects" of his activity. The prime example

---

[4] *Autobiography*, p. 95.

of such ignorance was his instigation of the death of Christ, which became the cause of our salvation. The Fathers say that the death of Christ was the hook by which he caught the devil.

Maisie Ward again: "He told Father O'Connor some years later that 'he had used the planchette freely at one time, but had to give it up on account of headaches ensuing. After the headaches came a horrid feeling as if one were trying to get over a bad spree, with what I can best describe as a bad smell in the mind.'"[5] And in a public talk on the defense of miracles, he made this confession of what happened when he was using the planchette:

> I in my boyhood worked with a planchette; and, though I am perfectly willing to admit that I may have gone mad for the time being, or that there were resources in my sub-consciousness I should never have imagined to exist; if anybody tells me that it was either cheating or done by my own will, I will say it is nonsense. The thing ran across a table a good deal longer than this by which I am standing, with a violent pull. There was something undoubtedly behind it, and it was not either of the two people working it. I simply put this in as my own personal testimony. I also came to the conclusion afterwards that it was a bad experiment, and I would not go on with it; and that is, I fear, faintly connected with the moral of the play [*Magic*] to which too much reference has been made.[6]

Did this memory come back to him while discussing miracles because it was a personal experience of *something happening outside the laws of nature*—"something undoubtedly behind it"? This was his encounter with Black Magic, which

---

[5] Ward, pp. 44-45.

[6] The Christian Commonwealth Co., Ltd. *Do Miracles Happen?* (London, 1914), p. 5. Quoted by Pearce, p. 204.

would afterwards supply the material for his play, *Magic*. And is he saying that the moral of *Magic* is to keep away from Black Magic?

In his much quoted article entitled "The Diabolist" he met a man whose mind was permeated with that "bad smell" as a permanent atmosphere, a man who was totally without principles or scruples:

> He had a horrible fairness of the intellect that made me despair of his soul. He only said, 'But shall I not find in evil a life of its own?' 'Do you see that fire?' I asked. 'If we had a real fighting democracy, someone would burn you in it; like that devil-worshipper that you are.' 'Perhaps,' he said, in his tired, fair way. 'Only what you call evil I call good.'[7]

As Chesterton was leaving the building where this meeting took place, he overheard the Diabolist and his acquaintance talking:

> I stopped, startled; but then I heard the voice of one of the vilest of his associates saying, 'Nobody can possibly know.' And then I heard those two or three words which I remember in every syllable and cannot forget. I heard the Diabolist say, 'I tell you I have done everything else. If I do that I shan't know the difference between right and wrong.' I rushed out without daring to pause; and as I passed the fire [fire place] I did not know whether it was hell or the furious love of God.[8]

Maisie Ward says "revulsion from the atmosphere of evil took Gilbert to no new thing but to a strengthening of old ties and a mystic renewal of them."[9] I wonder, though, if she does

---

[7] *Ibid.*
[8] *Ibid.*
[9] Ward, p. 46.

not significantly down play this youthful encounter with evil (since he had been innocent of evil before). I wonder if his meeting with the Diabolist was not some new and profound turning point in his life; the beginning of the radical cure for his skepticism; the foil that made his battlecry real. I venture this because the attitude of the Diabolist, as much as the headaches and bad smell from the planchette, "proved" to Chesterton the radical existence of evil and of the supernatural. In the very first sentence of the above-mentioned chapter he says what he is about to relate "has left in my mind forever a certitude upon the objective solidity of Sin."[10]

Significantly, Chesterton did not call this unfortunate young man the "Impressionist" or the "Decadent" or the "Sceptic" but the "Diabolist." He understood the encounter not only as being exposed to wrong ideas, but also as a meeting with the father of lies.

What Kind of Devils Were They?

The Coloured Lands contains some of Chesterton's earliest writings. For my purposes here "Half-Hours in Hades," written when he was only seventeen, holds a special fascination. Subtitled "An Elementary Handbook of Demonology," it antedates his actual encounter with evil spirits described above. The "Half-Hours" are very playful and humorous, too humorous, I believe, for the seriousness of the subject, even for Chesterton. (These notes seem like a kind of forerunner of *The Screwtape Letters*. Did C.S. Lewis know about them?) Chesterton does not treat devils quite so lightly after he met them. It seems he really believed in

---

[10] *Autobiography*, p. 81. These experiences of the "objective solidity of sin" tend to confirm what I argued for above, that he had a more than usual realization of sin.

them when he was seventeen; but perhaps they were still too much a part of his fairyland and world of innocence.

> In the autumn of 1890 I was leaving the Casino at Monte Carlo in company with an eminent Divine, whose name, for obvious reasons, I suppress. We were engaged in an interesting discussion on the subject of Demons, he contending that they were an unnecessary, not to say prejudicial, element in our civilization, an opinion which, needless to say, I strongly opposed. Having at length been so fortunate as to convince him of his error, I proposed to furnish him with various instances in which Demons have proved beneficial to mankind.[11]

Chesterton then proceeds to catalogue the various species of demons according to his creative imagination. He illustrates each of them.[12] I invite the reader to make her or his own interpretation:

> There is Tentator Hortensis, the Common or 'Garden' serpent, so-called because its first appearance in the world took place in a Garden. Since that time its proportions have dwindled considerably, but its influence and power have largely increased; it is found in almost everything.
>
> The Mediaeval Devil, Diabolus Faunalius. The Mediaeval Demon is, of all the species, perhaps the one with which we are most familiar. It is in a domesticated state the subject rather of playfulness and household merriment than of abhorrence. It is found at the present day as a general source of amusement, [but] it has of late somewhat failed to stir public interest.
>
> Diabolus Paradisi Perditi. Mr. J. Milton was the primary discoverer of this species and has discussed at some length

---

[11] G.K. Chesterton, *The Coloured Lands* (Sheed and Ward: New York, 1938), p. 60.

[12] *Ibid.*, pp. 65-72, and the other species mentioned here.

the leading characteristics of the species. This species is an inhabitant of warm latitudes like most of its kind, being originally found in the burning lakes and dark wildernesses of the most remote parts of the world.

The Red Devil, Diabolus Mephistopheles. It was discovered by Mr. Wolfgang von Goethe. In a domestic state this creature is playful and active, but mischievous and impossible to trust. The learned doctor found it a useful and entertaining companion for many years, but was finally persuaded to part with it. Its height is about six feet.

The Blue Devil, Caeruleus Lugubrius. Though formed by Super-Nature in their habits and exterior apparently for the filling of waste moors, mountains, churchyards and other obsolete places, these animals, like the Red Devil, have frequently been domesticated in rich and distinguished houses, and many of the wealthiest aristocrats and most successful men of commerce may be seen with a string of these blue creatures led by a leash in the street or seated round him in a ring on his own fireside. The noise made by this creature is singularly melancholy and depressing, and its general appearance is far from lively. But though less agile and intelligent than the Red Devil, the sobriety of its habits and demeanour have made it a suitable pet for the houses of clergymen and other respectable persons.

Caeruleus Lugubrius would be my choice for the species Chesterton met in the séances; I identify Diabolus Mephistopheles as the species working in "the Diabolist." "When the young student grows older," writes the seventeen year-old G.K., "he will meet with others in his own experience."[13] I must admit I was somewhat startled when I first read that the youthful Chesterton

---

[13] *Ibid.*, p. 72.

had drawn pictures of devils. Was this before or after his actual experience of them? Probably before.

Secrecy is of the Devil

These early imaginative depictions of the demons still seemed rather odd until I came across the following insights that express another driving force behind his writing and thinking: a horror of secrecy. We should "put things on the table," say what you really think, expose your inner world to the light. So he didn't conceal his early fascination with demons.

In the following passage he applies this line of thinking to thinking itself, to Christian and non-Christian art, and then to our major topic, talking about the devil. Generally, he thinks that *secrecy is of the devil*. But first about thoughts themselves:

> Whenever you hear much of things being unutterable and indefinite and impalpable and unnamable and subtly indescribable, then elevate your aristocratic nose towards heaven and snuff up the smell of decay [read "devil"]. It is perfectly true that there is something in all good things that is beyond all speech or figure of speech. But it is also true that there is in all good things a perpetual desire for expression and concrete embodiment; and though the attempt is always made to embody it is always inadequate, the attempt is always made. If the idea does not seek to be the word, the chances are that it is an evil idea. If the word is not made flesh it is a bad word.[14]

In another place he wrote: "I could fancy that men drew the Tempter with the curves of a serpent because they can be twisted into the shape of a question mark."[15] I interpret this to refer to

---

[14] G.K. Chesterton, "The Mystogogue," *A Miscellany of Men* (IHS Press: Norfolk, 2003).

[15] *The London Illustrated News*, Jan. 27, 1917.

the tempting question in the Garden, "Did God really say you must not…?" One of the devil's ploys is to ask questions which make us doubt the word of God, the trustworthiness of God.

Concealment of thoughts, in certain circumstances, can be a form of lying, used by the father of lies. He hates the light and the truth. So when he speaks it is often lying; and if he cannot or will not speak, or allow his followers to speak, the tactic is to remain silent and conceal one's plans, one's ideas. Above all he does not like to "put his cards on the table."

Chesterton then applies this line of thinking to art. It is not exactly germane to our topic, but it will lead into it—and meanwhile provide a bit of relief from the seriousness of our subject! As well, it will provide some consoling words for those who have been exposed to all the bad art of the Catholic world:

> Thus Giotto or Fra Angelico would have at once admitted theologically that God was too good to be painted; but they would always try to paint Him. And they felt (very rightly) that representing Him as a rather quaint old man with a gold crown and a white beard, like a king of the elves, was less profane than resisting the sacred impulse to express Him in some way. That is why the Christian world is full of gaudy pictures and twisted statues which seem, to many refined persons, more blasphemous than the secret volumes of an atheist. The trend of good is always towards Incarnation.[16]

Note the comment about the "secret volumes of an atheist." He says somewhere else that the Church never had secret societies, which were started by the Masons. The Church always tended to profess her faith openly. The word "martyr" means "witness." And the Lord said, "I have spoken openly to the world.

---

[16] *Ibid.*

I always taught in synagogues or at the temple, where all the Jews came together. I said nothing in secret."[17]

And now Chesterton applies this line of thinking to representations of the demons:

> But, on the other hand, those refined thinkers who worship the Devil, whether in the swamps of Jamaica or the salons of Paris, always insist upon the shapelessnesss, the wordlessness, the unutterable character of the abomination. They call him 'horror of emptiness,' as did the black witch in Stevenson's *Dynamiter*; they worship him as the unspeakable name; as the unbearable silence. They think of him as the void in the heart of the whirlwind; the cloud on the brain of the maniac; the toppling turrets of vertigo or the endless corridors of nightmare. It was the Christians who gave the Devil a grotesque and energetic outline, with sharp horns and spiked tail. It was the saints who drew Satan as comic and even lively. The Satanists never drew him at all.[18]
>
> "Whether or not there are devils, there most certainly are devil-worshippers."[19]

I don't know if the devil dislikes people drawing imaginative representations of him or not, or whether he ever inspires his followers to do so. Chesterton thinks not. But let me attempt an answer.

The following expression (from *Orthodoxy*) has been quoted so many times that I hesitate to use it again. But certain gems are oft repeated because they are gems. It's one of my favorite sayings that has recently been used under Chesterton's picture on a prayer

---

[17] John 18: 20.

[18] *Ibid.*

[19] *The Illustrated London News*, Sept. 22, 1917.

card invoking his prayerful intercession: "Angels can fly because they can take themselves lightly." To be able to *take oneself lightly*, to be able to laugh at oneself, is one of the healthiest of human traits. It is one of the signs of our transcendence, one of the "rumors of angels" in us, a kind of divine antidote to the exaltation of the ego.

Chesterton's following insight about the opposite of taking oneself lightly is less well known:

> Seriousness is not a virtue. It would be a heresy, but a much more sensible heresy, to say that seriousness is a vice. It is really a natural trend or lapse into taking one's self gravely, because it is the easiest thing to do. It is much easier to write a good *Times* leading article than a good joke in *Punch*. For solemnity flows out of men naturally; but laughter is a leap. It is easy to be heavy; hard to be light. Satan fell by the force of gravity.[20]

The devil fell because he took himself too seriously, that is, he did not acknowledge his dependence on God; he did not accept the obvious truth that he was not the center of the universe. Thus, taking himself so seriously, he doesn't have a sense of humor; and he certainly doesn't like to be laughed at. And those Christians—like Chesterton—who draw comic images of him, well, he probably doesn't like that either.

---

[20] *Orthodoxy*, p. 128. I don't know if the devil attempts to tell jokes, but Christopher Hollis said: "Just as General Booth refused to let the devil have all the best tunes, so Chesterton refused to let him have all the best jokes, and claimed that those who had the faith should also be allowed to have the fun." Quoted by Pearce, p. 58. And Chesterton had this to say about modern spiritualism: "Some people objected to spiritualism, table rappings, and such things, because they were undignified, because the ghosts cracked jokes or waltzed with dinner-tables. I do not share this objection in the least. I wish the spirits were more farcical than they are. That they should make more jokes and better ones, would be my suggestion. For almost all the spiritualism of our time, in so far as it is new, is solemn and sad. Some Pagan gods were lawless, and some Christian saints were a little too serious; but the spirits of modern spiritualism are both lawless and serious—a disgusting combination." Essay, "The Red Angel" in *Tremendous Trifles*.

The devil would rather remain unknown and—to use another over-quoted dictum—would rather convince people he doesn't exist. When he exposes himself he runs the risk of being rejected and expelled. Part of the official rite of exorcism is demanding to know the name of the demons. They resist such a disclosure. We have been informed by our scripture scholars that knowing the name of someone gives a certain power over that person. Frequently even the good angels refuse to give their names.[21]

The devil's abhorrence of the light is a theme in Chesterton's literature:

> 'I spare you,' said the Duke in a voice of inhuman pity. 'I refuse. If I give you the faintest hint of the load of horror I have to bear alone, you would lie shrieking at these feet of mine and begging to know no more. I will spare you the hint. You shall not spell the first letter of what is written on the altar of the unknown God.'[22]

And when the Duke tells Father Brown that he would die if he knew "the great Nothing," Father Brown simply says, "The Cross of Christ be between me and harm."

Patron Saint of Converts from Neo-Paganism

I am trying to demonstrate that Chesterton's encounter with evil, and especially with evil spirits, played a very important part in his understanding of reality. This influence appears again in the very autobiographical chapter "The World Inside Out" in *The Catholic Church and Conversion*:

---

[21] Judges 13:17
[22] *The Complete Father Brown*, "The Purple Wig," p. 253.

The word *Ecclesia* was only used of one reality, the Roman Catholic Church. When it fragmented into other 'churches' the Catholic Church did not become one of the churches: it remains the Mother Church which contains the essence of all the fragmented tendencies. A Protestant is a Catholic who has gone wrong. And, if you trace what is good in each of the Protestant churches, you will eventually find its source in the Great Church. This is true of Calvinism and Quakerism and all the other churches. And this discovery—that Catholicism contains all the truths—is perhaps the most towering intellectual transformation of all and the one that it is hardest to undo even for the sake of argument.[23]

But is this also true of many modern tendencies, that their origins can be found in the Great Church? Yes. Which two does he choose to speak about? Socialism and Spiritualism. He chooses to speak about these two because he was involved in them; and he experienced that they were heresies cut off from the full truth of Catholicism.

If Chesterton is ever canonized he would make a good patron saint for converts, since he had worked through all the tangles of the modern mind to reach the truth of Catholicism. He can help others do that. But he says that many modern *people are not thinking*. They are involved in "free thoughtlessness." Our society is not now embroiled in controversies over Calvinism or Albigensianism or the 29 Articles. We live in a neo-pagan society. Chesterton says he was really converted from *paganism*. Many more in our neo-pagan society will find him a good guide through this modern neo-paganism tangle.

He says in his concluding "Note on Present Prospects" that

---

[23] G.K. Chesterton, *The Catholic Church and Conversion* (The Macmillan Company: New York, 1929), p. 82.

modern people, especially the young, are not leaving the Church for an *ism*: "They abandon it for things and not theories; they leave it to have a high time. I know it is the cant phrase of the old rationalists that their [the youth's] reason prevents a return to the Faith, but it is false; it is no longer reason but rather passion."[24] He says such a revolt built on natural passion cannot last. We are in a sensate era. Chesterton knows how to get out of such a pagan situation. St. John Paul II said once—to encourage us—that Christianity was born in a pagan world. He was emphasizing that it is *not a challenge foreign to us* to penetrate a pagan society with the gospel: we did it once at the beginning of Christianity, and we can do it again. But it might take a few centuries!

Chesterton knew all about paganism, and would even prefer it to "little social sects." "I think I am the sort of man who came to Christ from Pan and Dionysus and not from Luther or Laud; that the conversion I understand is that of the pagan and not the Puritan."[25] He said that sometimes when he is in a melancholic and joking mood, and asks the question where he would go if he left the Church: "I certainly would not go to any one of those little social sects which only express one idea at a time. The best I could hope for would be to wander away into the woods and become a pagan. That at least would be beginning all over again."[26]

In speaking especially with young people over the years I have heard stories of some who had been shaken out of their irreligion and skepticism precisely by an experience of evil, or because they were finally disgusted with their paganism and passions.

---

[24] *Ibid.*, p. 113.

[25] *Ibid.*, p. 89.

[26] *Ibid.*

And it's true, as Chesterton said, most people do not really have profound intellectual problems about dogma. They have moral problems: the teaching of the Church is contrary to their desires and passions. Or they are simply ignorant of the gospel or of the Church. Or they are attracted to the "spiritual world" without any guidance. They think the "other world" is neutral.

I read about a new-ager who one night was winging out in his astral space ship. He had such an experience of evil that he saw in a flash that his whole involvement in the new age movement for the past fifteen years was one gigantic deception. This experience often leads people to a belief in the supernatural, and then to God, as it did, fortunately, for this young man. But not everyone is so blessed.

Modern neo-pagans dabble in pagan things just as Chesterton did. He can also witness to the fact that the spiritual world is not neutral. Many modern people are trying to re-invent religion, to "begin all over again." They could find guidance from Chesterton's own struggle with evil and paganism.

> To us, Spiritualists are men studying the existence of spirits, in a blind and blinding oblivion of the existence of evil spirits. They are, as it were, people just educated enough to have heard of ghosts but not educated enough to have heard of witches. If the evil spirits succeed in stopping their education and stunting their minds, they may of course go on forever repeating silly messages from Plato and doggerel verses from Milton.[27]

Chesterton "played around" in this world of spiritualism, just as so many moderns continue to do. He said when he was younger he had a revulsion for spiritualism, but he was "seduced by the world" into being a dilettante. If he had known about

---

[27] *Ibid.*, p. 83.

the Catholic Church and her teaching, he could have found the answers. He can witness, then, to the involvement of evil spirits in spiritualism, and demonstrate from his experience how what he calls here not the supernatural but the "unnatural" can lead to the Catholic faith.

Magic

Isn't it very significant that *Magic*, his first and the most popular of his plays, (even if he didn't consider it his best), is "arguing the case for an unfashionable belief in the reality of the power of evil."[28] Chesterton himself said about this play that "all the people in *Magic* are purposely made good: so that there shall be no villain, except the great invisible Villain." For his first play he could have chosen any number of topics, but the battle with the Evil One was foremost in his mind. I consider this an unambiguous and significant confirmation of how he understood what the battle was all about.

The Plot

A conjuror, a magician, has been invited to a wealthy home to perform his tricks. Chairs start moving around, and, most mysteriously of all, a red lantern across the field turns blue. Morris, the Americanized English sceptic, starts to go slightly ballistic because he can't figure out how these tricks are done. The other guests—his sister, a doctor, a rich uncle and an Anglican clergyman—beseech the conjuror to tell his secret so that poor Morris ("I don't believe in religion") can be "cured."

The conjuror, after much persuasion, agrees to reveal his secret: "Conjuror: 'I did it by magic.'[29] Doctor: 'But hang it all,

---

[28] Conlon's Introduction to "Magic" in *The Collected Work of G.K. Chesterton*, Vol. XI, p. 98.

[29] *Ibid.*, p. 136. Quotes are from this play.

there's no such thing.' Conjuror: 'Yes there is. I wish to God I did not know that there is.'" And then the Conjuror says to the equally sceptical Anglican clergyman (for which Chesterton was accused of a "sadly irreligious tendency" in his play):

> I want you to be martyred. I want you to bear witness to your own creed. I say these things are supernatural. I say this was done by a spirit. The doctor does not believe me. He is an agnostic; and he knows everything. The Duke does not believe me; he cannot believe anything as plain as a miracle. But what the devil are you for, if you don't believe in a miracle? What does your coat mean, if it doesn't mean that there is such a thing as the supernatural? What does your cursed collar mean if it doesn't mean that there is such a thing as a spirit? [Exasperated] Why the devil do you dress up like that if you don't believe in it? [with violence] Or perhaps you don't believe in devils?[30]

And in answer to Patricia's question as to how he did the tricks, he says: "How I did that trick? I did it by devils." And a few moments later: "In black blind pride and anger and all kinds of heathenry, because of the impudence of a schoolboy, I called on the fiends and they obeyed."

And the Conjuror decides to speak to the sceptic. "Doctor: Where are you going? I am going to ask the God whose enemies I have served if I am still worthy to save a child." The Conjuror leaves but then reappears at the garden doors: "Go back to hell from which I called you. It is the last order I shall give."

The Rev. Smith asks what he told Morris the sceptic: "I shall not tell you. 'Why not?'" "Because God and the demons and that Immortal Mystery that you deny has been in this room

[30] *Ibid.*

tonight. Because you know it has been here. Because you have felt it here. Because you know the spirits as well as I do and fear them as much as I do."

And it is likely that Chesterton was referring to his own headaches as a young man when he has the Conjuror say:

> I dabbled a little in table-rapping and table-turning. But soon had reason to give it up. Patricia: But why did you give it up? Conjuror: It began by giving me headaches. And I found that every morning after a Spiritualist séance I had a queer feeling of lowness and degradation, of having been soiled. It wasn't long before the spirits with whom I had been playing at table-turning, did what I think they generally do at the end of all such table-turning. They turned the table. They turned the tables upon me.[31]

We do not know what the Conjuror finally told Morris. Not the truth: he makes up a lie so that Morris can swallow it. He refuses to tell anyone else the lie, because then they would deny the experience of evil they have had, and tell his lie to others. Clearly, Chesterton is saying that belief in the devil is part of spiritual and mental sanity. Morris—and all the others—would really have been cured of their more deadly disease—skepticism—if they would believe in the devil.

Chesterton's vision of reality was born not only of mystical insights into the goodness of ordinary things like dandelions, or the splendor of the existence of wooden posts. It was also born out of a meeting with the Devil: "But I am not proud of believing in the Devil. To put it more correctly, I am not proud of knowing the Devil. I made his acquaintance by my own fault; and followed it up along lines which, had they been followed

---

[31] *Ibid.*, pp. 138-39.

further, might have led me to devil-worship or the devil knows what."[32]

The Father of Lies

And what was his experience of the essence of this Evil? "The only thing I will say with complete confidence about that mystic and invisible power is that it tells lies. The lies may be larks or they may be lures to the imperiled soul, or they may be a thousand other things; but whatever they are, they are not truths about the other world; or for that matter about this world."[33]

Could not *The Ball and the Cross* be the expression and foreshadowing of this aspect of his life's work, his combat with Satan? The Lord said that the devil is the father of lies. And St. John asks: "Who is the liar? It is the man who denies that Jesus is the Christ. Such a man is the antichrist."[34] And Origen, one of the great Church Fathers, simply called the Antichrist, "the Lie."

Chesterton experienced that there was an invisible power in the world that is a lie-telling thing. (As opposed to the Church, which he called a "truth-telling thing.") And the lie is that Jesus is not the Christ, and that the Church is not Christ's continuing presence. ("The Church really is like Antichrist in the sense that it is as unique as Christ. Indeed, if it be not Christ, it probably is Antichrist."[35])

---

[32] *Autobiography,* pp. 85-86. I must say that in reading a few commentaries on *Magic* I was surprised how little emphasis is given to what, in my view, is obviously the main point of the play—the reality of evil spirits. Most of the commentaries treat the literary aspects of Chesterton's style, how the play was accepted by the critics, and so on. But it's almost as if there is a hesitation, an unconscious denial, to face the central theme. It is curious!

[33] *Ibid.,* p. 87.

[34] 1 John 2:22.

[35] *The* Catholic *Church and Conversion* (The Macmillan Company, 1929), p. 67.

Chesterton's life's work, chillingly clarified by his encounter with the Devil, would be to fight against this lie about Christ and his Church under its multitudinous ancient and modern forms. The Antichrist, in John's theology, is anyone who denies that Jesus is God who has come in the flesh. *The Catechism of the Catholic Church* puts it thus: "The supreme religious deception is that of the Antichrist, a pseudo-messianism by which man glorifies himself in place of God and of his Messiah come in the flesh."[36]

Chesterton perceptively points out one of the great lies of the devil: "The Devil is he who says he is God. That is, he is one who says that his functions are infinite and cannot be judged."[37] The devil in his bravado blusters that he is some kind of equal to God, just as infinite and just as powerful. On the contrary, all we have to do is meditate on Christ's encounters with the devil in the gospel. There is no contest here: it is God verses a fallen angel. The Lord simply says, "Be quiet!" or "Be gone!" and that's the end of the pseudo-struggle. It is essentially a non-combat situation.

The splendor of the goodness and truth of the world also blazes more brightly if one believes in the reality of this Evil. Without this foil, life is melancholic, "an aching vacuum of joyless approval, dreary, a miserable truce." Paradoxically, Chesterton's zest for life also came from his meeting with Anti-life.

Belief in the Devil Makes You More Charitable

Awareness of the devil and his temptations is one of the factors behind Chesterton's celebrated charity towards his intellectual foes, towards everyone, really. He believed that erroneous ideas affected moral behavior, and that often people were not aware

---

[36] CCC, No. 675.

[37] *Daily Herald*, May 31, 1913.

that their ideas were erroneous. (He said there were two kinds of people: those who hold dogmatic positions consciously, and those who hold them unconsciously—like George Bernard Shaw.) What he's saying—and a whole modern school of psychology (Cognitive Therapy) is built on this theory—is that maybe people are grouchy because they harbor pessimistic ideas, not pessimistic because they are grouchy; maybe people are sad and unpleasant because they have fatalistic and harsh ideas, not harsh because they are unpleasant people. And so on.

The devil is the father of lies. If you believe that Satan is alive and active, tempting people with lies, you will be more charitable and compassionate. If we do not believe in the devil, we then naturally attribute all the evil in the world to human beings alone, and regard many of our fellow-creatures as, well, "fiendish," when they might actually be tempted or tormented victims. And, if we accept the reality of possession, this also will make us more charitable: "The assertion that a man is possessed of a devil is the only way of avoiding the assertion that he is a devil."[38] Of course, such compassion can be overdone. But it is a very common human opinion that there are evil things in the world of such magnitude (the Holocaust) that they can only be called devilish; and to say that there are no devils is really to conclude that all evil comes from human beings.

Discerner of Thoughts

The mothers and fathers of the desert were geniuses in discriminating among the multitude of thoughts in the mind—*logismoi*, they were called. They knew very well what this "new" school

---

[38] *The Illustrated London News*, April 28, 1917. I remember reading of a *New York Times* editorial when the Nazi extermination camps came to light. It was quite explicit in saying that there must be some other source of evil in the world to explain such monstrosities.

of psychology was discovering: that you can't really have a human action without a thought; and that your thoughts have a powerful effect on your being. In a celebrated conversation with his followers, St. Anthony said that true knowledge was the ability to discern between good and evil, that is, good and evil thoughts. He was saying that there are no more important discernments we can make.

Chesterton saw very clearly how intellectual error begets moral error, and he understood that this was his particular battle ground: "I have come to attach much more importance than most modern people do to the influence of intellectual error upon moral character; but for that very reason, I am readier to admit that gallant and glorious fight that is often made by moral character against intellectual error."[39] Chesterton believed that the devil was often the instigator of false ideas. (Ignatius of Loyola emphasized this in his Spiritual Exercises.)

In the opening paragraphs of "Demons and the Philosophers" in *The Everlasting Man*, Chesterton gives some truly penetrating insights as to just why the human race, down through the ages—and perhaps even more so in our own time—is drawn to fraternize with demons. His insights are on a more intellectual plane than would have been those of St. Anthony or St. Pachomius, but this is an essential part of Chesterton's real genius: he saw that bad, erroneous thinking is harmful. The demons may tempt us in a sensual way with imaginings of false delights so that we succumb to something sinful. But they can also tempt us with false ideas as *ideas*, which can then lead us to evil. A false idea is even more harmful than a moral fault, for wrong ideas beget moral faults. We know nowadays that false ideas are also bad for your psychological and physical health.

---

[39] "The Heresy of Hustle," p. 151.

(If Anthony didn't explicitly know the theory of psychosomatic medicine, he knew the results of holy thoughts in his own body: he lived to be 105 years old. And to his dying day he had all his own teeth and could walk 20 miles!) The charismatic heart of Chesterton's spiritual fatherhood is in this area of discerning false and harmful ideas.

One of Chesterton's insights about the human race and demons that should give us more than pause is that communication with them is a phenomenon which occurs not for the most part in a so-called primitive stage of a civilization but rather *in its developed stages*:

> In the accounts given us of many rude and savage races we gather that the cult of demons often came after the cult of deities, and even after the cult of one single and supreme deity.
>
> And all over the world the traces can be found of this striking and solid fact, so curiously overlooked by the moderns who speak of all such evil as primitive and early in evolution, that as a matter of fact some of the very highest civilizations of the world were the very places where the horns of Satan were exalted, not only to the stars but in the face of the sun.[40]

---

[40] *The Everlasting Man*, pp. 118-19. The Canadian philosopher Charles Taylor, in his magisterial *A Secular Age* (The Belknap Press of Harvard University: Cambridge, Mass., and London, England, 2007), has offered insights into how Satanism has increased in our "advanced civilization." At the Reformation there was a widespread rejection of the Church's sacramental life, a "disenchantment" of life. One consequence of this was: "If we are not allowed to look for help to the sacred, to a 'white' magic of the church, then all magic must be black. All spirits now are ranged under the devil, the one great enemy. Even supposedly good magic must really be serving him. In a sense, the demons get concentrated, even as the positive energy of God is concentrating out of its dispersal in charged objects and church magic. There is one enemy, THE devil, Satan." pp. 80-88. Example: I read once, in extreme evangelical literature in the United States, that all so-called apparitions of the Virgin Mary are diabolical. Without the Church's belief in, and discernment about, supernatural occurrences, everything "unnatural" is attributed to Satan.

Reading the opening sections of "Demons and Philosophers" should be very sobering for our "civilized" nations. We, especially in North America, are a very practical, pragmatic people. If a mountain is in the way of a desired highway, we just remove it. Technology is the new metaphysical mind-set: do A and B and presto! C happens. We desire to *get things done*, and we know how to do them better than any other civilization in the history of the world. Chesterton says that one of the temptations/attractions for invoking evil spirits is precisely their *practicality*:

> To start with, some impulse, perhaps a sort of desperate impulse, drove men to the darker powers when dealing with practical problems. There was a sort of secret and perverse feeling that the darker powers would really do things; that they had no nonsense about them. And indeed that popular phrase exactly expresses the point. The man consulting a demon felt as many a man felt in consulting a detective, especially a private detective; that it was dirty work but the work would really be done. The demon really kept his appointments and even in one sense kept his promises.[41]

This belief that the demons are practical and can "get things done" for us is also a lie: "God is a workman and can make things. The Devil is a gentleman and can only destroy them."[42] The demons cannot really "co-create with God" as we can. Their activity is totally negative and unsubstantial. Relying on them to help us is an illusion.

> With the idea of employing the demons who get things done, a new idea appears more worthy of the demons, of making oneself fit for their fastidious and exacting society. With the

---

[41] *Ibid.*, pp. 118, 121.

[42] "The Face of Brass" in *The Collected Works of G.K. Chesterton*, Vol. XIV, p. 735.

appeal to the lower spirits comes the horrible notion that the gesture must not only be very small but very low, of an utterly ugly and unworthy sort. Sooner or later a man deliberately sets himself to do the most disgusting thing he can think of. It is felt that the extreme of evil will extort a sort of attention or answer from the evil powers under the surface of the world.[43]

Traditionally we understand evil spirits as haters of humankind, envious of our redemption by Christ. We are enjoying the light of Christ; they still live in the darkness they have chosen, and they are diabolically jealous. Thus, black magic becomes inhuman. Chesterton attributes cannibalism and human sacrifice, especially of children, to demons. And when we consider the plague of abortion in our own time, can we fail to see the demons' hatred of the human race at work: "But without dwelling much longer in these dark corners, it may be noted as not irrelevant here that certain anti-human antagonisms seem to recur in this tradition of black magic. There may be suspected as running through it everywhere, for instance, a mystical hatred of the idea of childhood."[44]

Chesterton is grateful that Rome defeated Carthage, and that Christianity did not have to contend with the Carthaginian child-eating Moloch, but instead with the milder Zeus and Saturn and Apollo. It is mostly in our own time that the perverse spirit of Moloch lures millions to commit abortion. And isn't it significant that when the Child of Peace entered upon his earthly pilgrimage the demons unleashed their fury in the destruction of the *children* in Israel? I highly recommend this chapter in *The Everlasting Man* as Chesterton's most extensive and penetrating treatment of the influence of demons upon civilizations.

---

[43] *The Everlasting Man*, p. 121.

[44] *Ibid.*, p. 122.

The Devil Can Quote Scripture

It is an ancient truth that the devil attempts to use scripture to his advantage. (Recall the temptations of Christ in the wilderness.) The desert fathers and mothers, even though they lived alone, were dependent on the Church for her guidance; and their deep prayer life put them in touch with the Holy Spirit whom Jesus said would help us understand the scriptures. Perhaps it has already been done, but a collection of Chesterton's interpretations of scripture texts would be a fascinating study. But the devil can be involved as well in "explaining" the scriptures to those he is tempting. Chesterton:

> The devil can quote Scripture for his purpose; and the text of Scripture which he now most commonly quotes is, 'The Kingdom of heaven is within you.' That text has been the stay and support of more Pharisees and prigs and self-righteous spiritual bullies than all the dogmas in creation; it has served to identify self-satisfaction with the peace that passes all understanding. And the text to be quoted in answer to it is that which declares that no man can receive the kingdom except as a little child. What are we to have inside is a childlike spirit; but the childlike spirit is not entirely concerned about what is inside. It is the first mark of possessing it that one is interested in what is outside. The most childlike thing about a child is his curiosity and his appetite and his power of wonder at the world. We might almost say that the whole advantage of having the kingdom within is that we look for it somewhere else.[45]

---

[45] G.K. Chesterton, *What I Saw in America* (Hodder and Stoughton: London, 1922), p. 142. I wish to offer my perspective to this remark of Chesterton's. That there is something divine in us (2 Peter 1:4) is one of the great revelations of the New Testament. His diatribe is directed against those who use this scriptural passage to emphasize the world inside to the neglect of the world outside. His mysticism (Cf. *The Tumbler of God*) is that of the child who sees God in the wonder of the world.

This text is more appropriate for my book on Chesterton's mysticism: he thought there was too much preoccupation with the interior world among the mystics and among many Christians; and that the inner world became more real than the outer world. I cite it here as an example from Chesterton of how Satan can distort the scriptures; in this case, mischievously withdraw people from the battles of the world by a misguided absorption with the "kingdom within." This highlights our need for help in discerning the interpretation of scripture for our personal lives. Theresa of Avila lists seven different kinds of false peace! We can misuse scripture without any help from the bad guys!

The Modern World "Rediscovers" the Demonic

In an issue of *Time* magazine not too long ago there was an article on the rise of belief in Satan. One of Chesterton's themes is that the modern world keeps "discovering" things that the Church has known for 2,000 years. Take the demonic, for example.

Nobody believes any more the fantastic tale of St. George and the Dragon. But suppose, says Chesterton, just suppose, by way of example, someone did believe it and went to the traditional site of this mythological battle to get proof. He finds "on that very field of combat the bones of a gigantic monster, or hieroglyphics representing maidens being sacrificed to such a monster. He has not found a single detail directly in support of St. George, but he has found a very considerable support of St. George and the Dragon."[46]

A modern example of what Chesterton is driving at here is the Star of Bethlehem. Nobody believes anymore in the

---

[46] G.K. Chesterton, *The New Jerusalem* (Hodder and Stoughton LTD: London, 1920), pp. 170-71.

fantastic story of the Star of Bethlehem. It's only a romantic and beautiful literary touch to the birth of the Savior of the world, and that's all. But suppose, just suppose, someone did believe it, and set out to prove it. And he came across—which is an actual fact—astronomical Chinese charts at the time of Christ, showing that three planets converged in the heavens at that time. It has never happened before and will never happen again. Such a convergence would have radiated an unusually bright and new star in the sky. It doesn't "prove" that this is what the Magi saw, but... modern research is uncovering things which lend unexpected weight, and a rational basis, to the "myths" of old.

So too in this area of the supernatural and the demonic: "There has been a return of mysticism without Christianity. Mysticism itself has returned, with all its moons and twilights, its talismans and spells, and brought with it seven demons worse than itself."[47] The problem is that we now have the demons without the Redeemer.

Chesterton mentions one area in particular where the demons have showed up: in our excursions into the vast interior spaces of the psyche. It is not only the Pentecostals who have rediscovered the demons, but the psychologists:

> Psychological study has brought us back into the dark underworld of the soul, where even identity seems to dissolve or divide, and men are not even themselves. Dual personality is not so very far from diabolical possession.
>
> And if the dogma of sub-consciousness allows of agnosticism, the agnosticism cuts both ways. A man cannot say there is a part of him of which he is quite unconscious, and only conscious that it is not in contact with the unknown. He cannot say there is a sealed chamber or cellar under his

[47] *Ibid.*, pp. 177, 180.

house, of which he knows nothing whatever; but that he is quite certain that it cannot have an underground passage leading anywhere in the world.[48]

Chesterton, of course, is not calling all modern psychology demonic. But he is saying that we get into very deep waters here; and, if they are unconscious depths, we cannot know whether or not we are opening underground passages to the demons. (I'll be considering the goblins and their underground habitats in *The Princess and the Goblin*.) It's been said of the Germans (read Freud and Nietzsche) that they dive deeper but come up muddier! This could apply to some psychologists.

Another area where the demonic is appearing with still greater clarity is in "a mass of fiction and fashionable talk of which it may truly be said that we miss in it not demons but the power to cast them out. It combines the occult with the obscene; the sensuality of materialism with the insanity of spiritualism."[49]

What we really lack here is not the supernatural but the *healthy supernatural*. "We have not found St. George, but we have found the Dragon. We have found, in the desert, the bones of the monster we did not believe in because they are there. Christian demonology has survived in the form of heathen demonology."[50]

"I Saw Satan Fall like Lightning"

Many people point to Christ as a great poet or prophet or moralist. In many ways he is very much alive to modern people. But if anyone really set off to discover Christ—read the gospels as if for the first time with unprejudiced eyes (which is how Chesterton

[48] *Ibid.*, p. 177.
[49] *Ibid.*, p. 178.
[50] *Ibid.*, p. 179.

tried to present Christ in *The Everlasting Man*)—what would he or she discover?

> It is that the exorcist towers above the poet and even the prophet; that the story between Cana and Calvary is one long war with demons. He understood better than a hundred poets the beauty of the flowers of the battle-field; but he came out to battle. And if most of his words mean anything they do mean that there is at our very feet, like a chasm concealed among flowers, an unfathomable evil.
>
> The language of the Gospel seems to me to go much more singly to a single issue. The voice that is heard there has such authority as speaks to any army; and the highest note of it is victory rather than peace. When the disciples were first sent forth with their faces to the four corners of the earth, and turned again to acclaim their Master, he did not say in that hour of triumph, 'All are aspects of one harmonious whole,' or 'the Universe evolves through progress to perfection,' or 'all things find their end in Nirvana' or 'the dewdrop slips into the shining sea.' He looked up and said, 'I saw Satan fall like lightning from heaven.'"[51]

The Devil and Father Brown

Chesterton's "inspiration" for the Father Brown stories was also, in a significant manner, connected with Satan's presence in the world; or rather, with a priest's awareness of such a presence. In a conversation with Fr. O'Connor, Chesterton said he was about "to support in print a certain proposal in connection with some rather sordid social question of vice and crime." Fr. O'Connor disagreed with publishing it.

---

[51] *Ibid.*, p. 185.

And, merely as a necessary duty and to prevent me from falling into a mare's nest, he told me certain facts he knew about perverted practices which I certainly shall not set down or discuss here. I have confessed on an earlier page that in my own youth I had imagined for myself any amount of iniquity; and it was a curious experience to find that this quiet and pleasant celibate had plumbed those abysses far deeper than I. I had not imagined that the world could hold such horrors.[52]

Chesterton does not say specifically that what Fr. O'Connor related to him was about devilish practices, but the context lends itself to this interpretation. Chesterton refers to his earlier chapter "when he met the devil"; also, "such horrors" seems to refer to more than mere human depravity. And, a few passages later, he will refer to "Satanism."

When he and Fr. O'Connor returned to the house they entered into conversation with two hearty and naive young Cambridge undergraduates about music and art and related matters. When Fr. O'Connor left, these budding scholars began talking somewhat in this manner: "It's all very well to like religious music and so on when you're all shut up in a sort of cloister and don't know anything about real evil in the world." And then, Chesterton relates what was, for him, the original inspiration for Fr. Brown:

> To me, still almost shivering with the appalling practical facts of which the priest had warned me, this comment came with such a colossal and crushing irony, that I nearly burst into a loud harsh laugh in the drawing room. For I knew perfectly well that, as regards all the solid Satanism which the priest knew and warred against with all his life, these two Cambridge

---

[52] *Autobiography*, p. 317.

gentlemen (luckily for them) knew about as much of real evil as two babes in the same perambulator. And then sprang up in my mind the vague idea of making some artistic use of these comic yet tragic cross-purposes, and constructing a comedy in which a priest should appear to know nothing and in fact know more about crime than the criminals.[53]

This "inspiration" for the Fr. Brown stories is another strong argument to tone down the metaphorical interpretations of Satan in the stories and give more weight to explicit references to the father of lies.

"The Man Who Was Evil"

And what was his frame of mind at the time of writing *The Man Who Was Thursday*? "I was still oppressed with the metaphysical nightmare of negations about mind and matter, with the morbid imagery of evil, with the burden of my own mysterious brain and body; but by this time I was in revolt against them; and trying to construct a healthier conception of cosmic life."

People were trying to figure out what the novel was all about. If they had paid attention, Chesterton said, to the subtitle—"A Nightmare"—they might have answered some of their own questions.

People were especially intrigued by the symbolic identity of "the monstrous pantomime ogre who was called Sunday."[54] Some thought "he was meant for a blasphemous version of the Creator." But Sunday "is not so much God, in the sense of religious or irreligious, but rather Nature as it appears to the pantheist, whose pantheism is struggling out of pessimism."[55]

---

[53] *Ibid.*, p. 318.

[54] *Ibid.*, p. 103.

[55] *Ibid.*

But the meaning of Sunday goes through a metamorphosis even in the writing. "Even in the earliest days and even for the worst reasons, I already knew too much to pretend to get rid of evil. I introduced at the end one figure who really does, with a full understanding, deny and defy good."[56] Chesterton emphatically denies he arrived at this conception from priests: "I had learned it from myself. I was already quite certain that I could if I chose cut myself off from the whole life of the universe."[57] This unnerving comment is reminiscent of what the Diabolist said to him: "But shall I not find in evil a life of its own?" Chesterton said that this "quiet conversation was by far the most terrible thing that has ever happened to me in my life."

Chesterton's writings about the saints reveal his conceptions about sanctity. And he strove, I believe, to learn himself from their lives so he could be holy too. As a rather stout journalist of Fleet Street he could not exactly identify with the emaciated hermit in the Egyptian desert. But, like Anthony, he could fight lies, especially any lie that pretended to contradict the truth of the gospel. Chesterton, through experience, knew that the demons were real, as real as they were for Anthony in his cave. And, like Anthony, he would fight them and win.

In the 21st century we want to recall Chesterton's frequent distinction between a radical who believes in the goodness of the world, and therefore fights for it, and the mere conservative who believes that the world is bad and so allows it to go to the dogs, or go to hell. As the culture continues to deteriorate around us there is an enormous danger of becoming *mere* conservatives, of pulling up the drawbridges and waiting for the end. If I remember correctly, Dante said that the greatest

---

[56] *Ibid.*, p. 104.

[57] *Ibid.*

punishments are reserved for those who take no stand, remain neutral, lukewarm.

The true radical continues to fight for goodness and truth because she or he believes they are worth fighting for. "And in your muddy souls you can't see that the one perfectly divine thing, the one glimpse of God's paradise given on earth, is to fight a losing battle—and not lose it."[58] Until the Lord comes, we want to try and make this world as beautiful as we can for his arrival, and not have him arrive on top of a garbage heap. The victory may be inconclusive in this world, but the oil in our lamps is this zeal and courage in the battle we have waged for truth and goodness.

Von Balthasar gives a powerful interpretation of the reality of this battle with Satan which is very germane to the theme of this book:

> St. Paul does not suggest that Satan, the 'god of this world'[59], and the powers associated with him, have been simply dethroned: Christ's war against these powers continues through world time.[60] There *is* a region outside the community of salvation, a region subject to Satan [1 Cor. 5:5; 2 Cor. 2:11; 1 Tim. 1:20]. Indeed, Satan can act as tempter and persecutor even within the inner realm of salvation [1 Cor. 7:5; 2 Cor. 11:14; 12:7; 1 Th. 2:18]. Thus Christians are entangled in a struggle against superhuman powers and cannot survive without 'the whole armor of God' [Eph. 6:10-18].[61]

---

[58] From his play, "Time's Abstract and Brief Chronicle," *The Collected Works of G.K. Chesterton,* Vol. XI, p. 62.

[59] 2 Corinthians 4.

[60] 1 Corinthians 15:24.

[61] *Theodrama,* Theological Dramatic Theory IV: the Action (Ignatius Press: San Francisco, 1994), pp. 180-181.

> St. Paul envisages a final battle that will take place when 'the secret power of godlessness' which is 'already at work,' will no longer be subject to any restraint; 'the coming of the lawless one by the activity of Satan will be with all power and with pretended signs and wonders, and with all wicked deception for those who are to perish, because they refused to love the truth and so be saved. *Therefore God sends upon them a strong delusion, to make them believe what is false* [2 Th. 2:7-11]. [emphasis mine][62]

This teaching will serve as a good introduction to my next two chapters. And it emphasizes that the heart of the battle is for *truth*. Chesterton's charism is at the heart of the battle—the pugnacious struggle against the father of lies.

Gilbert, pray that we are not cowards, afraid of the war with evil. Pray that, in this Third Millennium, we don't become bored and melancholy and dreary and discontented and miserable because we are afraid to fight, even if the battle at times seems hopeless. O Gilbert, pray that, along with all the other necessary virtues, we may have a pugnacious belief in the father of lies, and the courage to face him, keep our joy, and thus see more clearly the splendor of truth in our own blazing apocalypse.

[62] *Ibid.*

CHAPTER FOUR

THE HOLY WAR AND THE BALL AND THE CROSS

At the beginning of this chapter it will be helpful to make several important distinctions between the Antichrist, the beast, and the dragon in scripture:

> The Book of Revelation clearly distinguishes between the three key figures who will arise in opposition to Christ and the Church at the end of time: the Antichrist, the beast, and the dragon (or serpent). Whereas the Antichrist is a man, the beast is a political power that brings war to the earth. It is the dragon who is identified with the devil. There is no ambiguity or confusion in revelation between these three distinct realities.[1]

In the two novels I will be comparing to Chesterton's *The Ball and the Cross* (*B&C*), the main character is the Antichrist. However, in *B&C*, Professor Lucifer is obviously not meant to be the Antichrist but Satan: "Now I know who you really are. You are not God. You are not one of God's angels. But you once were."[2] Wood also sees him thus: "The cleft-bearded Dr. Lucifer represents the mutinous archangel in modern form."[3] My point of comparison is that all three novels are in the apocalyptic genre; and while two represent the Antichrist, and Chesterton's the Devil, both dark characters employ similar tactics for their deceptions.

---

[1] Jose Antonio Fortea, *Interview with an Exorcist* (Ascension Press: West Chester, Pennsylvania: 2006).

[2] G.K. Chesterton, *The Ball and the Cross* (John Lane Company: New York, 1909).

[3] Wood, p. 133.

It seems that Chesterton knew of these distinctions. He wrote in 1906, during the period he was writing *B&C*, that "the worst result of popular evolutionism has been this: It has substituted the Beast for the Devil."[4] He is saying, I believe, that in modern conflicts, the world has forgotten the involvement of Satan in evil regimes. Thus, no attention is given to the spiritual combat against the "powers and principalities." Everything is seen in purely political terms.

The Devil as Muse

A fascinating book that will serve as a kind of background to this chapter is *The Devil as Muse* by Fred Parker.[5] I say "kind of" because his main thesis does not really apply to Chesterton. Parker states it thus: "This book explores the notion of a radical tension between the ethical and the aesthetic—the virtuous philosopher and the chameleon poet—through the idea of the Devil as Muse, *whereby the creative artist is seen as diabolically sponsored or inspired.*" (emphasis mine) If I understand him correctly, his book is about how the two artists he has chosen to consider—Blake and Byron—are inspired, not by the traditional devil who is always the Adversary, but by a devil with more "positive features" according to the authors own imaginative conceptions. Not only are they "inspired" by a heterodox conception of the devil, but Parker also attempts to show that these authors *personally identified with their more sympathetic understanding of the devil*, and that the authors' personalities were influenced by their conceptions.

---

[4] *Daily News*, February 3, 1906.

[5] Fred Parker, *Blake, Byron, and the Adversary* (Baylor University Press, 2011), p. 4. Quotes in the following paragraphs are from Parker unless otherwise noted.

To bring out his muse theory he contrasts the demons of Blake and Byron with Milton's demon in *Paradise Lost*. Milton clothed the devil with the traditional characteristics. However, he laid the groundwork for other more "sympathetic" understandings of the devil: "It was Milton in *Paradise Lost*, more decisively than anyone else in the history of literature or art who first re-imagined the Evil One in such a way as to make possible full imaginative relations with him." (Recall Chesterton's description above in *The Coloured Lands* of Milton's role in making the Diabolus Paradisi Perditi more popular.)

Byron and Blake tried to argue that Milton was on Satan's side so that they could then use him as a predecessor for their more sympathetic relationship with the Adversary. (Most scholars have vigorously denied this interpretation.) However, it is true that "Milton brought the Devil into being, made him there for us, in a way that the monsters in the medieval frescoes, or the malignant demons of the late-medieval imagination, could never be." Milton made Satan "the most interesting and engaging character in *Paradise Lost*." The reason was because "he gives Satan *depth*, which we do not get from the other devils, or from God, or from Adam and Eve." In short, Milton paved the way for treating Satan as a real personality, and thus opened the way for giving him a character after the artist's own liking.

I will give just one example from Parker to emphasize the difference between this Muse's influence on Blake and Byron, and Chesterton's relationship to Professor Lucifer in *B&C*. Byron seems to be the quintessential example of the author's thesis that the personality of Satan took over the artist Byron. If true, I found what happened to Byron quite frightening.

"Byron's protagonists in his poems are darkly heroic figures who share many characteristics with Milton's 'archangel ruined.' They are fallen beings—but tremendous in their fallenness."

Indeed, most of the poems that made Byron famous are inescapably self-referential; the potency of his 'Satanic' heroes was hugely enhanced by his own reputation. 'Mad, bad, and dangerous to know,' he was understood, like his creations, to walk on the wild side. He had travelled in the exotic East, lived the life of the libertine, taken the radical side of politics, driven his virtuous wife into separation, and was rumored to have slept with his half-sister; now he lived in exile in Italy, where he was said to indulge in all manner of sexual license, and kept company with the atheist Shelley. His club foot suggested some more essential deformity, or brand of distinction, half-concealed like the Devil's cloven hoof. A plausible anecdote relates that '[he] used to declare that he was a fallen angel, not symbolically but literally, and told Annabella [his wife] that she was one of those women spoken of in the bible who are loved by an exile from Heaven.'

In *Twelve Types* Chesterton wrote of Byron:

But through all this his sub-conscious mind was not that of a despairer; on the contrary, there is something of a kind of lawless faith in thus parleying with such immense and immemorial brutalities. It was not until the time in which he wrote 'Don Juan' that he really lost this inward warmth and geniality, and a sudden shout of hilarious laughter announced to the world that Lord Byron had really become a pessimist.

The truth is that Byron was one of a class who may be called the unconscious optimists, who are very often, indeed, the most uncompromising conscious pessimists, because the exuberance of their nature demands for an adversary a dragon as big as the world.[6]

---

[6] G.K. Chesterton, *Twelve Types* (IHS Press: Norfolk, 2003).

So did Byron create this dragon as the muse which rode him?

Wood has this quote from Chesterton: "Popular tales about bad magic are specially full of the idea that evil destroys personality. In all such distinctive literature the denial of identity is the very signature of Satan."[7] One wonders if Byron did not actually lose his personality in giving himself over to his muse of Satan.

Parker then quotes from a reviewer of one of Byron's poems: "The mind of the noble author has been so far tinged by his strong conception of the Satanic personage, that the sentiments and reflections which he delivers in his own name have all received a shade of the same gloomy and misanthropic colouring."

After reading this book I was in even greater amazement at our hero, Chesterton. His aesthetic drive was as strong as Blake's or Byron's or Goethe's. And yet, by the grace of God, he kept his aesthetic genius in harmony with his ethics and personal life. In many artists their aesthetic flames have burned at the center of their lives to become almost a god, a religion. (Paul Tillich defined religion as whatever is at the center of one's life.) I stand in awe at Chesterton's balance. He was, perhaps, more familiar with the real Satan than either Blake or Byron, and yet he never allowed his imaginative conceptions of Satan to take over his personality.

But, as usual, Chesterton himself has the best insights into his own literary psychology. In his essay, "The Nightmare," he says "that there is nothing so delightful as a nightmare—when

---

[7] "Wishes," in *The Uses of Diversity*, p. 116. In another personal communication to me (July 24, 2012), Ralph Wood perceptively said: "Be sure to note that the Devil, as the cleverest beast of the field, always impersonates, since he has no real personhood; for to be a person is to dwell wholly in God. Christ is the only true person." This reflection will be especially relevant for the impersonations Professor Lucifer takes on in *The Ball and the Cross*. Besides impersonation, then, the devil's main thrust is to *destroy personality* since he has lost his and doesn't want anyone else to have one.

you know it is a nightmare."⁸ Chesterton is commenting on some of the monsters depicted in the Book of Revelation.

> I like those monsters beneath the throne very much. It is when one of them goes wandering in deserts and finds a throne for himself that evil faiths begin, and there is (literally) the devil to pay—to pay in dancing girls or human sacrifice. As long as those misshapen elemental powers are around the throne, remember that the thing that they worship is the likeness of the appearance of a man.
>
> That is, I fancy, the true doctrine on the subject of Tales of Terror and such things, which unless a man of letters do well and truly believe, without doubt he will end by blowing his brains out or by writing badly. Man, the central pillar of the world, must be upright and straight; around him all the trees and beasts and elements and devils may crook and curl like smoke if they choose. All really imaginative literature is only the contrast between the weird curves of Nature and the straightness of the soul. Man may behold what ugliness he likes if he is sure that he will not worship it; but there are some so weak that they will worship a thing only because it is ugly. These must be chained to the beautiful. It is not always wrong even to go, like Dante, to the brink of the lowest promontory and look down at hell. It is when you look up at hell that a serious miscalculation has probably been made.
>
> Therefore I see no wrong in riding with the Nightmare. We will rise to that mad infinite where there is neither up nor down, the high topsy-turveydom of the heavens. I will answer the call of chaos and old night. *I will ride on the Nightmare; but she shall not ride on me.*⁹ [emphasis mine]

---

⁸ G.K. Chesterton's essay "The Nightmare." Read Books Online. Web. 23 Apr. 2014.
⁹ *Ibid.*

This needs no comment. Chesterton was not afraid of Professor Lucifer as a muse, as long as "he did not ride on me." How tragic that Byron didn't have Chesterton's wisdom and Christian virtue!

The Holy War

William Oddie's article, "Chesterton at the Fin de Siecle: Orthodoxy and the Perception of Evil,"[10] introduced me to another source of Chesterton's thinking about personal evil; it was also a very welcomed confirmation of the main thesis of my book! Oddie's article was a foreshadowing of his classic referred to above (*Chesterton and The Romance of Orthodoxy*). I am not concerned with Oddie's treatment of the origins of Chesterton's battle with the decadence of his age as represented by Wilde, Pater and associates, but with another inspiration for Chesterton's fighting spirit against evil treated in *The Chesterton Review* article.

Oddie found, in Chesterton's dedication of *The Man Who Was Thursday* to his closest friend, E.C. Bentley, another clue to his fighting spirit. We have seen the entire dedication, but this is the relevant line here: "We have seen the City of Mansoul, even as it rocked, relieved." Oddie says that this refers to Bunyan's second spiritual allegory, *The Holy War*, where the hosts of the devil besiege the City of Mansoul. "What appears to have interested Chesterton was that it is about the struggle for the salvation of a whole culture as much as for the salvation of individual souls."[11] The following quote sums up my whole thesis:

> And it is at this point, it seems to me, that we find an important key to understanding Chesterton's own feelings about those

---

[10] *The Chesterton Review*, Vol. XXV, No. 3, August 1999, pp. 329-343.

[11] *Ibid.*, p. 336.

years in which he was coming to literary maturity. It is not simply that the *fin de siecle* was a period in which men had gone mad; it was a time when they were possessed by a great evil, in which the city, like Mansoul, was besieged by the hosts of the devil. It is here, I must suggest, that we must look for the real origins of Chesterton's mature philosophy of life. *My proposal is that Chestertonian orthodoxy begins with a vision not simply of unorthodoxy but of positive evil* [emphasis mine], with a nightmare which fades with the light of day, but which is never finally forgotten. He has become what Walter de la Mare was to call him decades later: a 'Knight of the Holy Ghost, the mills of Satan keeping his lance always in play.' The sequence is this: the perception of evil leads to the perception that it is heresy that has led to the evil and that it is only the huge sanity of orthodoxy that will overcome the madness of evil. Life for Chesterton has now become, to evoke Bunyan again, a Holy War.[12]

Although *B&C* didn't appear until 1910, Chesterton began serializing it in 1905, and therefore was no doubt thinking about it before then, around the turn of the century. And just as we were bombarded around the year 2,000 with innumerable apocalyptic and *fin de siecle* pronouncements on every topic, and using every conceivable literary genre to express "the end," so were writers around the year 1900 articulating imaginative end time themes.

Bunyan's *Holy War* was a new text for me, so I perused it with an eye for what Chesterton might have gotten out of it. One passage especially caught my attention, and forms a fitting

---

[12] *Ibid.*, p. 336-37. Significantly, in relation to my theme, it was Frances, Chesterton's wife (Cf. Pearce, p. 480), who included de la Mare's verse about the "mills of Satan" on Gilbert's memorial card. It indicates that she also understood her husband's lifetime battle was contending against the "mills of Satan."

introduction to one of the basic themes in B&C which is of particular interest to me: the devil.

In *The Holy War*, *diabolus* and his infernal friends, after they had been expelled from the King's realm, are discussing how to re-enter the City of Mansoul. Here is their third option, which they eventually adopt:

> Whether they had best to show their intentions, or the design of his coming, to Mansoul, or no. This also was answered in the negative, because of the weight that was in the former reasons, to wit, for that Mansoul were a strong people, a strong people in a strong town, whose wall and gates were impregnable, (to say nothing of their castle,) nor can they by any means be won but by their own consent. 'Besides,' said Legion, (for he gave answer to this,) 'a discovery of our intentions may make them send to their king for aid; and if that be done, I know quickly what time of day it will be with us. Therefore let us assault them in all pretended fairness, covering our intentions with all manner of lies, flatteries, delusive words; feigning things that never will be, and promising that to them that they shall never find. This is the way to win Mansoul, and to make them of themselves open their gates to us; yea, and to desire us too to come in to them. And the reason why I think that this project will do is because the people of Mansoul now are, every one, simple and innocent, all honest and true; nor do they as yet know what it is to be assaulted with fraud, guile, and hypocrisy. They are strangers to lying and dissembling lips; wherefore we cannot, if thus we be disguised, by them at all be discerned; our lies shall go for true sayings, and our dissimulations for upright dealings. What we promise them they will in that believe us, especially if, in all our lies and feigned words, we pretend great love to them, and that our design is only their advantage and honour.' Now there was

not one bit of a reply against this; this went as current down as doth the water down a steep descent.[13]

"Our lies shall go for true sayings, and our dissimulations for upright dealings." This is the tactic Professor Lucifer will use in *B&C*. Perhaps Chesterton was partly inspired by his reading of *The Holy War* when he was penning *B&C*.

Of course, there are a variety of interpretations of *B&C*. This is only right and proper. Wood has a chapter on *B&C*, but he treats it mostly from the point of view of the meaning of toleration. It makes excellent reading for the whole issue of political correctness today. However, he mentions not at all my theme of the Antichrist. I take comfort about this omission from his opening comments to Chapter Seven, *The Man Who Was Thursday*: "There is nothing approaching a consensus about the meaning of MT. All great works of art are subject to diverse even contradictory interpretations."[14] There is no one interpretation of great works of art. Flannery O'Connor called it the x factor. "There is no such x factor to be found in MT." I would apply this to B&C as well, and to all of Chesterton's novels. I believe Wood would also.

My contention is that *B&C* is the most concentrated expression of one very important aspect of Chesterton's life's work—his pugnacious battle with diabolus - and especially with the devil as the *father of lies*. To repeat Oddie again: "Chestertonian orthodoxy begins with a vision not simply of unorthodoxy but of positive evil, with a nightmare which fades with the light of day, but which is never finally forgotten." Oddie, in *The Romance of Orthodoxy*, does not apply this important insight to *B&C*, but that is my intent here.

---

[13] John Bunyan, *The Holy War* (Christian Classic Ethereal Library).

[14] Wood, p. 187.

Emile Cammaerts says that "the Master in *The Ball and the Cross* is called pointedly Professor Lucifer, and we had better leave it at that." I'm not going to "leave it at that." This novel fits in perfectly well with my theme because it is about fighting Satan and his lies. It is Chesterton's most extensive treatment of Satan's techniques of deception in the modern world. Chesterton knew all about these devilish strategies. In his account of his own conversion he wrote: "Many converts, far more important than I, have had to wrestle with a hundred devils of howling falsehood."[15] The *B&C* is a prime example of how pervasive the battle with *Satan* was in Chesterton's writing, whether explicitly expressed or not. My thesis is that this battle with Satan is always in the background of Chesterton's mind. (Oddie: "A nightmare which fades with the light of day, but which is never finally, forgotten.") He may be using metaphors when he uses words like "satanic," "hellish," and "diabolical," but the reality of Satan is what keeps his jousting realistic and alert.

Blessed John Henry Newman, Robert Hugh Benson, and Vladimir Soloviov

I was on my way out the door to give some retreats. I took *B&C* off the shelf and noticed that I had first read it in 1983. I remembered there were many profound ideas in it, but little action. "I don't pretend to get half of it—but it's beautiful, isn't it—and oddly written." Thus a pencil note at the very end of a first edition of *B&C* I was reading. Also, I didn't think that I "got half of it," and for some reason I couldn't remember how the book ended. I wondered what I would get out of it now. What I got out of it this time around was very much colored by the

---

[15] *The Catholic Church and Conversion*, p. 28.

fact that I had just finished reading Newman's *The Patristical Idea of Antichrist* written in 1872.[16]

Chesterton's novel struck me now as being about the Antichrist; or, at least, Professor Lucifer as the spirit of the Antichrist. An awareness of, and belief in, the coming of the Antichrist is an aspect of the Church's understanding of Satan's activity in the end times.

The turn of the 20th century inspired at least two important works about the Antichrist. Vladimir Soloviov (1853-1900), considered by many to be the greatest Russian religious thinker of all time, wrote his famous *Three Conversations* in 1900, just a few months before he died. It contains his story of the Antichrist.[17]

Robert Hugh Benson's *The Lord of the World* (1907) was the other apocalyptic novel of the time.[18] We *do know* that Chesterton read this book. In *The Thing* he wrote: "[Civilization] will sooner or later try to supply the need of something like a Papacy; even if it tries to do it on its own account. That will be indeed an ironical situation. The modern world will have to set up a new anti-Pope, even if, as in Monsignor Benson's romance, the Anti-Pope has rather the character of an Antichrist."[19] What is remarkable (as we shall see) is the similarity in the understanding of the Antichrist/Satan in these three works.

At the end of his treatise Newman quotes favorably from a certain Bishop Horsley who wrote, in 1834:

---

[16] John Henry Newman, *Discussions and Arguments On Various Subjects,* 1872.

[17] Vladimir Soloviov, *War, Progress, and the End of History,* "Three Conversations, Including a Short Story of the Antichrist" (Lindisfarne Press, 1990).

[18] Robert Hugh Benson, *The Lord of the World* (Dodd, Mead and Company: New York, 1946).

[19] *The Thing* (Sheed & Ward: New York, 1930), pp. 245-46.

> The Church of God on earth will be greatly reduced, as we
> may well imagine, in its apparent numbers, in the times of
> Antichrist, by the open desertion of the powers of the world.
> This desertion will begin in a professed indifference to any
> particular form of Christianity, under the pretense of universal
> toleration; which toleration will proceed from no true spirit
> of charity and forbearance, but from a design to undermine
> Christianity, by multiplying and encouraging sectaries. For
> governments will pretend an indifference to all, and will give
> a protection in preference to none.[20]

This is an accurate and prescient description of the character and method of the Antichrist in all three works we will be considering: the Antichrist, benignly and paternalistically, pats all religions and sects on the head, asking them all to get along nicely with one another: "All religions are good, respected, and tolerated. Just don't get into any arguments about 'dogmas' because there is no truth or substance behind such doctrines. Actually, there are no absolute truths at all, so why argue about them. Just be respectful to one another and we'll all get along fine." I believe *B&C* is Chesterton's vision of this benign and relativistic attitude of the Antichrist/Professor Lucifer who will proclaim that since there are no absolute truths, there is no rationale for fighting over ideas, much less fighting a duel.

B&C is a long story containing many of the lies Chesterton fought all his life. He is one of the great chivalrous white knights fighting the lies against the gospel in the battlefield of the mind. The beginning of our first parents' downfall was entertaining a doubt about God's command: "Did God really say you must

---

[20] Newman, p. 106. Is this not an accurate description of how the "powers of the world" today are treating Christianity? Wood expands on this theme with great perception and at length.

not eat...?" Throwing such questions at us, making us doubt God's veracity and trustworthiness, is one of the devil's tactics.

The next step was accepting a falsehood in their minds, an idea contrary to our loving Father's command: "You will not die. For God knows that..."[21] Satan suggested that God was not to be trusted, that he was playing games. The acceptance of that terrible falsehood led to the disobedient act. At the heart of the battle, for Chesterton, is refuting lies that cause all human tragedies, since the acceptance of a lie was at the heart of the original catastrophe.

As mentioned at the beginning of this chapter, in the theology of the Fathers and in Catholic theology generally, the Antichrist is not Satan but someone completely under his influence; perhaps someone really possessed. For my purposes it's inconsequential whether Professor Lucifer is Satan or the Antichrist; they are interchangeable as far as their purpose and methods are concerned. I will simply equate Professor Lucifer with Benson's Lord of the World and Soloviov's Julian Felsenburgh so I can compare the three works together as *fin de siecle* literature. All three are incarnations of the father of lies against whom Chesterton was battling. The three stories are similar as being apocalyptic literature.

Dale Ahlquist wrote:

> Exactly 35 years after Chesterton died the Archbishop of Venice wrote him a letter. He wanted to express his grateful agreement with the profound truths conveyed in Chesterton's novel, *The Ball and the Cross*, particularly the idea that when people set out to destroy the cross, they end up destroying everything else, and doing it in the name of 'rationalism.' Chesterton never wrote back to Archbishop Albino Luciani,

---

[21] Genesis 3:1-4.

but we can speculate that they had an illuminating discussion on the matter when they presumably met just seven years later, when Luciani entered eternity after a mere 33 days as Pope John Paul I.[22]

The Plot of the Ball and the Cross

The fiery Catholic MacIan smashes the office window of the newspaper *The Atheist* after reading therein a blasphemous statement that the Blessed Virgin Mary was just like all the other virgins of mythology, conceiving "by some profligate intercourse between God and mortal." The editor of *The Atheist*—Turnbull—comes out, understandably, to see why his window was smashed. "Because it was the quickest cut to you," says MacIan.[23] "Stand up and fight you crapulous coward. You dirty lunatic stand up, will you? Have you any weapons here?" They agree to a duel because both are passionate about their ideas and believe they are worth fighting for. Hovering above the whole episode is Professor Lucifer in his spacecraft. Lingering in a cell in a loony bin throughout most of the novel is the white-haired monk Michael, "the happiest man in the world," the Christ-figure, and who, at the end of the novel, is urged by MacIan, "Father, come out and save us all."

MacIan certainly has the right ideas, but his method of fighting is wrong: he wants to spill blood through a duel. For all his fiery virtues he eventually comes to see that a physical duel is not the Christian way to defend Our Lady's honor. Father Michael's way is the best. At the end both MacIan and Turnbull

---

[22] Dale Ahlquist, "Lecture 15: The Ball and the Cross," *Chesterton 101 Lecture Series*. http://www.chesterton.org/lecture-15/. 01 Mar. 2014.

[23] *The Ball and the Cross*, p. 36. All subsequent quotations are from this novel unless otherwise noted.

go through a change of heart towards one another, coming even to *like* one another:

> Some new and strange thing was rising higher and higher in their hearts like a high sea at night. It was something that seemed all the more merciless, because it might turn out an enormous mercy. Was there, perhaps, some such fatalism in friendship as all lovers talk about in love? Did God make men love each other against their will?

I will not be concerned with this change of heart in MacIan and Turnbull, although it was one of Chesterton's great personal virtues to really love and respect his intellectual opponents and to become friends with them. I will be principally concentrating on the dominant theme which is *the battle for the human mind*, for Christian truth, over against any idea or attitude which seeks either to deny it or render it harmless by tolerating it as one of many "spiritual paths."

MacIan is a type of those who believe there is truth, and that it is worth fighting for. He is also a type of "the common man" who possesses the basic human and Christian wisdom which too many ideologues, such as Turnbull, know nothing about. Other types of this common wisdom are Pierre Durand, who "was merely a man," and his marvelous daughter Madeleine, "whose silent energy went into her prayers," and who "was not in the least afraid of devils. I think they were afraid of her." "They neither of them believed in themselves; for that is a decadent weakness." On one level, then, the novel is about the wisdom of simple people taught by God, in contrast to the ideas of the over- or under-educated, whichever way you want to look at them.

CROSS PURPOSE OR BALLED UP

The key to the novel is in the early discussion between Professor Lucifer and Father Michael over the symbolism of the ball and the cross atop St. Paul's Anglican Cathedral in London. "The globe is reasonable," says the satanic Professor, "the cross is unreasonable. The globe is inevitable. The cross is arbitrary. The globe is at unity with itself; the cross is primarily and above all things at enmity with itself. The cross is the conflict of two hostile lines, of irreconcilable directions." Professor Lucifer would put the ball on top of the cross. That would "sum up my whole allegory." Only one problem with that, Father Michael suggests humbly, "I mean it would fall down." For Father Michael, human life *is* a contradiction—like a cross: "We like contradictions." Life's problems are not resolved by simply saying everything is rational, inevitable, and, underneath, a unity—like a ball.

From the point of view of method, the "ball-way" is expressed in the encounter with the "Peacemaker" who says, in a discussion about murder: "Well, we won't quarrel about a word." To which MacIan responds with his very Catholic and gospel mind:

> 'Why on earth not?' said MacIan, with a sudden asperity. 'Why shouldn't we quarrel about a word? What is the good of words if they aren't important enough to quarrel over? Why do we choose one word more than another if there isn't any difference between them? If you called a woman a chimpanzee instead of an angel, wouldn't there be a quarrel about a word? If you're not going to argue about words, what are you going to argue about? Are you going to convey your meaning to me by moving your ears? The Church and the heresies always used to fight about words, because they are the only things worth fighting about.'

All of England is trying to stop the duel because it implies that MacIan and Turnbull are *actually taking the God question seriously*. "We are fighting about God; there can be nothing as important as that." The novel is about these two fanatical men who actually see a contradiction in their ideas—a "cross-purpose"—and believe in these ideas passionately enough to fight over them.

This disturbs everyone in England for whom reality is, at bottom, reasonable, inevitable, a unity—in short, a ball. "No, no," say our two warriors, "people certainly *do not* agree about the nature of Reality, and it's crucial to argue about the differences." Turnbull says:

> Try and understand our position. This man and I are alone in the modern world in that we think that God is essentially important. I think He does not exist; that is where the importance comes in for me. But this man thinks that He does exist, and thinking that very properly thinks Him more important than anything else. Now we wish to make a great demonstration and assertion—something that will set the world on fire like the first Christian persecution. If you like, we are attempting a mutual martyrdom.

Christians throughout the ages have given their lives for Jesus Christ because they believed something about him that clashed with the ideologies of their persecutors. This conflict was expressed in *words and ideas*: "Caesar is not divine; Christ is divine. Allegiance to Christ is above allegiance to Hitler, Lenin, or Mao." Such allegiance was at the heart of their understanding of the Lord's words, "Whoever loves father or mother more than me is not worthy of me; and whoever loves son or daughter more than me is not worthy of me."[24] Words express our visions of reality. If our visions clash, so must our words. We do not all mean the same thing; it is not true that *only our words are different!*

Actually, it is also true that the modern world believes in fighting over ideas. Since the French Revolution more blood has been spilt over the clash of secular ideologies than by past "wars of religion." These very "wars of religion" turned many sincere and thoughtful men away from religion: "Religion is the problem, so let us build society on enlightened reason."

Now, in the last two centuries, we know that reason is even less capable of achieving peace and security in society than religion. We do not, of course, wish to return to religious wars. But we do want to return to the intellectual passion for religious ideas. The modern attitude in the *B&C* is that, because Christianity and religion are dead and have "failed," it is really silly and useless to argue over such ideas. To argue over other ideologies, yes, but not over realities that don't exist—like God and the Incarnation. The "Ball Attitude" desires to wish this conflict away; the "Cross Attitude" desires to unmask error with the revolutionary truth of Jesus Christ: "Do not suppose that I have come to bring peace to the earth. I did not come to bring peace but a sword."[25]

That Christianity and its adherents are insane is a major theme of Benson's novel as well. Pope Sylvester (the last saint on the liturgical calendar) is in hiding in Nazareth. He is reflecting on the state of the gospel in the world:

> It was a lost cause for which He suffered; He was not the last of an august line, He was the smoking wick of a candle of folly;

[24] Matthew 10:37.
[25] Matthew 10:34.

He was the *reductio ad absurdum* of a ludicrous syllogism based on impossible premises. He was not worth killing, He and His company of the insane—they were no more than the crowned dunces of the world's school. Sanity sat on the solid benches of materialism.[26]

The Peacemaker

We turn now in *B&C* to some of the attitudes that seek to dismiss any serious debate between the gospel and the modern world. We might label the first attitude "Peace and Love At All Costs." Chesterton calls his character that embodies this attitude "the Peacemaker." The gentleman's voice that personifies this mental malady is "too polite for good manners. His attire was all woven according to some hygienic texture which was absolutely necessary even for a day's health." Regarding this absurd duel of MacIan and Turnbull over the existence of God, the Peacemaker appeals to their "higher natures": "I must and will stop this shocking crime. It is against all modern ideas. It is against the principle of love. We have no dogmas, you know. There's something in what Shaw teaches about no moral principles being quite fixed."

Needless to say, our two convinced dogmatists can't wait to get out of this "peaceful"—not to say comatose—man's presence. He doesn't understand a thing about Christianity and the Church whose sacred dogmas clash with falsehood like the swords of our warriors. MacIan sums up what capitulation to this attitude would mean:

> My soul said to me: 'Give up fighting, and you will become like That. Give up vows and dogmas, and fixed things, and

[26] Benson, p. 45.

The Holy War and The Ball and the Cross

you may grow like That. You may learn, also, that fog of false philosophy. You may grow fond of that mire of crawling, cowardly morals, and you may come to think a blow bad because it hurts, and not because it humiliates. Oh, you blasphemer of the good, an hour ago I almost loved you! But do not fear for me now. I have heard the word Love pronounced in *his* intonation; and I know exactly what it means.'

This exemplifies the many varieties of approaches to "peace" in the world that sacrifice truth. One form this takes in our time is the New Age Movement: "Let us all just get in touch with the harmonizing forces of the cosmos, and all our dogmatic stances will blend into the universal synthesis." Soloviov, in his work on the Antichrist, pinpoints this same attitude in the book published by the Antichrist as the new bible for the world:

> His famous work [was] entitled *The Open Way to Universal Peace and Prosperity*. It was a work that embraced everything and solved every problem. It joined a boundless freedom of thought with the most profound appreciation for everything mystical. Every thinker and every man of action could easily view and accept the whole from his particular individual standpoint without sacrificing anything to the *truth itself*.[27]

Soloviov's Antichrist also held a world congress "for the unification of all cults," and people filed in to the tune of a newly composed song, "The March of Unified Humanity." (Something about a one-world religion today! And Soloviov wrote this in 1900!)

Chesterton wrote *B&C* in the first decade of the 20th century when his Peacemaker spoke of "no moral principles being quite fixed." Many years later, in *G.K.'s Weekly*, June 19, 1926, he said:

---

[27] Soloviov, p. 179.

The grand heresy of the last days [note the apocalyptic reference] will simply be an attack on all morality, but especially on sexual morality. I say that the man who does not perceive this fails to discern the signs of the times. Tomorrow's folly will not come from Moscow but rather from Manhattan—even more than what has been seen on Broadway up to date—which is beginning to come to Piccadilly.[28]

This attitude had become so pervasive in the 20th century that St. John Paul II wrote an encyclical *The Splendor of Truth*, exposing the moral relativism of the modern world. (And Benedict XVI famously coined the expression *the dictatorship of relativism*.) "The Peacemaker," then, personifies a superficial love at the expense of truth. After being totally repulsed and nauseated by the Peacemaker, MacIan turns to Turnbull and shouts, "On guard!"

Although the Peacemaker's intellectually soupy approach to truth has deceived millions in our modern world, it actually is not a great temptation for our two knights in their passion for ideas. They still believe that truth exists. The real test for each of them comes in their dreams in which Professor Lucifer uses his most subtle approaches, adapted to each one's major weakness.

The Dream of Turnbull

If Professor Lucifer cannot convince Turnbull that there is no truth, or that it's "unloving" to be passionate about ideas, he will then seek to foster his—Turnbull's—passion for his error. Lucifer's purpose is ultimately chaos and discord, and it's irrelevant to him how it is achieved.

---

[28] Quoted by Ian Boyd, "Chesterton: A Prophet for Today," in *Christ to the World*, No. 1, 1989, p. 34.

Turnbull, who has "the masculine but mirthless courage of the atheist," meets Professor Lucifer in a dream. The Master of Deceit appears in a "lean brown body bare to the belt of his loose white trousers. The face was strong, handsome, and smiling, with a well-cut profile and a long cloven chin."

Professor Lucifer adopts the friendly, slap on the back, comrade-in-arms attitude. He addresses our heroic but confused warrior as "Jimmy," and, being asked what he wants, says, with unusual satanic honesty, "I want *you*." The ruse is that, really, they are on the same side: "I want exactly what you want. I want the Revolution." And with the intellectual arrogance and blindness of those who are convinced that religion must be destroyed (but who are not too clear about the program to replace it), Turnbull exults: "The Revolution—Yes, that is what I want right enough—anything, so long as it is a Revolution."

Professor Lucifer appeals to Turnbull's misguided zeal by telling him that he has been chosen—and what a bolstering of the ego to be chosen!—to belong to the truly greatest of all Revolutions: "We are going to destroy the Pope and all the kings. All the great rebels have been very little rebels. They have been like fourth-form boys who sometimes venture to hit a fifth-form boy. That was all the worth of their French Revolution and regicide. The boys never really dared to defy the schoolmaster. 'Whom do you mean by the schoolmaster?' asked Turnbull. 'You know whom I mean.'" My own opinion is that "the schoolmaster" is the Pope: "It is the last war, because if it does not cure the world forever, it will destroy it."

Chesterton wrote *B&C* during the height of the Modernist controversy. In an exchange with Robert Dell, a convert to Catholicism with strong modernist leanings, and who had launched a bitter attack on Pope Pius X using all the old Protestant clichés, Chesterton wrote:

Why cannot he argue with the Pope without playing to the No-Popery gallery? He says a man becoming a Catholic and is converted to be saved 'the trouble of thinking.' Why, quite so, and the 'Mass is a Mummery,' and 'the Pope is the Beast in Revelations.' Unless Modernism has some strange and softening influence on the brain, Mr. Dell *must* know better. He must know whether men like Newman and Brunetiere left off thinking when they joined the Roman Church.[29]

A few years later (1911), speaking to the University students at Cambridge, he said: "I can assure you, and I would prove it to you if I had time, that the Popes have done a hundred times more for Liberty than any of the Protestant Churches ever had."[30] In both Soloviov and Benson, the Pope of Rome is the ultimate counter force to Satan and his Antichrist. Chesterton, who was not to become a Catholic until 1922, prophetically saw that Professor Lucifer *must* destroy the Pope—"the schoolmaster"—if his domination is to succeed.

What a profound prophetic vision we have here from Chesterton! Fueled by such ideologies as Nietzsche's Death of God, the Superman, atheistic Communism, and purely secular humanism, the "Great Revolution" of the early part of the 20th century set out to destroy religion, and especially the Catholic Church. This movement is still with us, though perhaps not as blatant and physically violent as it was in Mexico, the Soviet Union, Spain and China. Former dictators of the 20th century

---

[29] Fr. Ian Boyd, "Chesterton's Anglican Reaction to Modernism," *The Chesterton Review*, Vol. XV, Nos. 1-2, Feb/May, 1989, pp. 21-33. Chesterton's article, from which this quote is taken, was called, "The Staleness of Modernism," and it shows a profound understanding of Catholicism.

[30] *Ibid.*, p. 32. I was at a meeting a number of years ago and one of the participants had just returned from a seminar at the UN on moral issues. Someone said there, speaking of John Paul II, "this Pope must be destroyed."

really believed that Catholicism could be destroyed; more recent despots know that it cannot be: "Let us then marginalize its influence by legally ostracizing it from the public square." Such is the growing modern form of persecution.

Many in our time still see the Pope and the Catholic Church as one of the greatest obstacles to progress and human development. Catholicism is not the strong meat needed by the supermen of the future: "'This Catholicism is a curious thing,' said the man of the cloven chin. 'It soaks and weakens men without their knowing. Do you want to be taken to a monastery with MacIan and his winking Madonnas?'"

Turnbull might have enlisted into the Great Revolution to destroy the schoolmaster if Professor Lucifer had not made a tactical error. Turnbull was still enough of a human being, still unconsciously retained enough of his Christian heritage, to detect it. He still believed in the rights of the individual, and in the basic sanctity of human life. Professor Lucifer exposes too much of his hidden agenda by saying: "Yes, indeed, Life is sacred—but *lives* are not sacred. We are improving Life by removing lives. Can you, as a free-thinker, find any fault in that?"

Well, yes, as a matter of fact, Turnbull can. It is too much for him. He still believes in the dignity of the person and in individual freedom.

The same theme again is in Benson. Pope Sylvester, in the catacombs of Nazareth, is reading a life of the Lord of the World, Julian (as in Apostate) Felsenburgh:

> His [Felsenburgh's] spirit was in the world; the individual was no more separate from his fellows; death no more than a wrinkle that came and went across the inviolable sea. For man had learned at last that the race was all and self was nothing; the cell had discovered the unity of the body; even the greatest thinkers declared the consciousness of the individual

had yielded the title of Personality to the corporate mass of man—the restlessness of the unit had sunk into the peace of a common Humanity.[31]

This approach to world peace is even more prevalent today, and assumes many forms. Communism did not believe in the individual: Millions were sacrificed to reach the utopian ideal. The abortion mentality does not believe in the sanctity of life in the womb: babies can be sacrificed to the ultimate perfection of the race, commonly understood as the more convenient—read selfish—well-being of the couple. Euthanasia advocates do not believe in the dignity of suffering. Eugenic engineering, in all its forms, still seeks to sanitize the world to achieve, in the appealing and dazzling vision of Professor Lucifer, "the golden girls and boys leaping in the sun." They are all based on the theory that to arrive at the perfection of the human race, we can trample on *individual lives.*

At the time he was beginning to write *B&C*, Chesterton wrote in the *Daily News* (February 18, 1905): "We shall see wars and persecutions of a kind the world has not yet known. People shed tears for the victims of Bonner or Claverhouse whereas they should weep for themselves and for their children."[32] Fr. Ian Boyd comments: "The people to whom he first addressed his message would have realized him only in hope and not in fact. He had already spoken clearly of the return of infanticide which would accompany the new paganism. He was an isolated voice of protest at the time against the eugenic ideology then in fashion."[33]

Turnbull opts not to join in this Great Revolution. He leaps from the spaceship.

---

[31] Benson, p. 74.

[32] *Modernism*, p. 33.

[33] *Ibid.*

The Dream of MacIan

Professor Lucifer's approach to MacIan had to be more subtle than his approach to Turnbull, as the former was a zealous believer, and, even more irritating, a Catholic. So there are no anti-God, anti-Church, anti-Pope tactics. Lucifer seeks to enlist MacIan's zeal in the cause of *law and order* so dear to the Catholic heart and ethos.

"'Evan,' said the voice, 'your sword is wanted elsewhere.' 'Wanted for what?' asked the young man. 'For all you hold dear. For the thrones of authority and for all ancient loyalty to law.' 'Who are you?' 'I must not say who I am until the end of the world; but I may say what I am. I am law.'"

In this dream Lucifer appears quite beautiful, with "the face of a Greek god"—beautiful and pleasant like the Antichrists of Benson and Soloviov. "There was nothing to break this regularity except a rather long chin with a cleft in it." The cleft, of course, symbolizes his cleavage from God. And again, as in the temptation to Turnbull, there is here also the chivalrous appeal to enlist MacIan's sword in a holy war. All the kings have returned. Let us join the rule of law and order and restore peace to the world.

In a striking similarity to this "Catholic temptation" in *B&C*, Soloviov's Antichrist tempts Catholics in exactly the same way.

The Emperor calls for a congress to meet in Jerusalem on September 14 (the Feast of the Exultation of the Cross) devoted to the unification of all cults. Pope Peter II leads the Catholics, Elder John the Orthodox, and Professor Pauli the Evangelicals. The Emperor tempts the Orthodox with a promise to preserve all their traditions; and the Evangelicals will have unlimited resources to research the scriptures. He tempts the Catholics thus:

> Dear Christians! I know that for many, and not the least among

you, the most precious thing in Christianity is the *spiritual authority* with which it endows its legal representatives. I, therefore, most solemnly declare that it is pleasing to our autocratic power that the Supreme Bishop of all Catholics, the Pope of Rome, be henceforth restored to his throne in Rome with all former rights and privileges belonging to this title and chair given at any time by our predecessors, from Constantine the Great onward.[34]

Sounds good! Only one condition: "I wish to receive from you only your inner heartfelt recognition of myself as your sole protector and patron."[35] Many applaud the decree, but Pope Peter and others see the trap in the Emperor's offer.

Doubts arise in MacIan as well. He takes offense when he sees a soldier striking an old man because he is not moving fast enough along the street. MacIan thinks this is unjust. "We attach great importance to discipline," says the Professor. "Discipline," says MacIan, "is not so important as justice." "I am not sure," retorts Lucifer, "that I agree with your little maxim about justice. Discipline for the whole society is surely more important than justice to an individual."

This spirit of the Antichrist—justice without mercy—takes this same shape in *The Lord of the World*. Mabel, the wife of a high official of the New Humanity, begins to have doubts when she sees a mob kill Catholics who are resisting the New Order of Worship:

> It was incredible, she told herself, that this ravening monster, dripping with blood from claws and teeth that had arisen roaring in the night, could be the Humanity that had become her

---

[34] Soloviov, pp. 180-81.
[35] *Ibid.*

God. She had thought that revenge and cruelty and slaughter to be the brood of Christian superstition, dead and buried under the newborn angel of light, and now it seemed that the monsters yet stirred and lived.[36]

He husband reassures her that this is only a step on the way to the unity of the world.

Professor Lucifer's temptation does not succeed. The proverbial cat is out of the bag. MacIan challenges his law and order approach to peace:

> 'Who and what are you?' 'I am an angel.' 'You're not a Catholic. Why, you great fool!' cried MacIan, 'did you think I would have doubted only for that rap with a sword? I know that noble orders have bad knights, that good knights have bad tempers, and that the Church has rough priests and coarse cardinals; I have known it ever since I was born. You fool! You had only to say, "Yes, it is rather a shame," and I should have forgotten the affair. But I saw on your mouth the twitch of your infernal sophistry; I knew that something was wrong with you and your cathedrals. Something is wrong; everything is wrong. You are not an angel. That is not a church. It is not the rightful king who has come home.'

'And how do you know,' he said, 'how to you know that I am not God?' MacIan screamed. 'Ah!' he cried. 'Now I know who you really are. You are not God. You are not one of God's angels. But you were once.'

And MacIan, too, leaps from the spaceship.

There are further parallels with Soloviov's Antichrist. At the

---

[36] Benson, p. 259.

International Congress for the United States of Europe, the Antichrist's manifesto closes with the rousing words:

> 'Nations of the World! I give you my peace. The promises have been fulfilled! An eternal universal peace has been secured. Every attempt to destroy it will meet with determined and irresistible opposition. This unconquerable, all-surmountable power belongs to me. Henceforth, no country will dare say 'War' when I say 'Peace!' Peoples of the world, peace to you!'[37]

All three accounts have a prophetic statement about the Antichrist's dominion: It will be an iron fist in a satin glove. Fascist regimes of iron law and order did arise to force people to be at "peace." But the spirit behind these regimes is not that of the King of Peace. It is the spirit of the Antichrist.

Martin Gardner in "Levels of Allegory in *The Ball and the Cross*" mentions three levels. His second level comes closest to the particular interpretation I am emphasizing here. He says:

> On a second level of allegory *The Ball and the Cross* is clearly intended to mirror the conflict between Augustine's 'City of God,' which for Chesterton was the Catholic Church, and the 'City of Man' which is under the control of Satan. If one is a conservative Catholic, one can interpret the novel as being about the conflict between the Church and Satan—a conflict destined to last until the end of the world.[38]

At the turn of the century the basic conflict between good and evil was becoming glaringly clear. Nietzsche declared that God was dead. (In 1900 God declared that Nietzsche was dead!) In that same year, the last of *his* life, Soloviov wrote his story of the Antichrist. Atheistic Communism was soon to sweep over

---

[37] Soloviov, p. 172.

[38] *The Chesterton Review*, Vol. XVIII, No. 1, pp. 40-78.

Holy Russia. Modernism, the font of all heresies, would be condemned in 1907. And Pope St. Pius X (1903-1914) would frequently allude to Satan and his powers at work in the modern world: "There has never been a time when this watchfulness of the supreme pastor was not necessary to the Catholic body; for, owing to the efforts of the enemy of human race, there has never been lacking men speaking perverse things";[39] "The authors of this war [against the Catholic Church] boast that they are waging it in love of liberty. In this lie too [they] resemble their father, who was a murderer from the beginning, and when he speaketh a lie, he speaketh of his own, for he is a liar' (John 8:44), and raging with hate insatiable against God and the human race."[40]

---

[39] Pius X, *Pascendi Gregis,* September 8, 1907.

[40] Pius X, *Communium Rerum,* April 21, 1909.

CHAPTER FIVE

THE FEARFUL AND HATEFUL ANTICHRIST OF BENSON AND SOLOVIOV

For those who had eyes to see, the time was ripe for some literary expression of this apocalyptic battle between Christ and Antichrist, between the Church and Satan. I am certain that neither Chesterton nor Benson could have read Soloviov's *Story of the Anti-Christ*. Chesterton began serializing *B&C* in 1905 and 1906 in *The Commonwealth*. Benson's novel was published in 1907. The first major work in the West on Soloviov was Michel d'Herbigny's Vladimir Soloviev, *Un Newman Russe*, 1911. It was translated into English in 1918. It's possible that both Chesterton and Benson knew of Vladimir Soloviov *after writing their books*. However, the Soloviov's *Story* was not in d'Herbigny's translation. All the more surprising, therefore, are the amazing similarities to Soloviov in their imaginative accounts of the personality traits of the Enemy.

I have mentioned that Chesterton read Benson; and Benson, of course, knew of Chesterton:

> 'Have you read,' he asks in this year [1905], 'a book by G.K. Chesterton called *Heretics?* If not, do see what you think of it. It seems to me that the spirit underneath it is splendid. He is not a Catholic, but he has the spirit. He is so joyful and confident and sensible! One gets rather annoyed by his extreme love of paradox; but there is a sort of alertness in his religion and in his whole point of view that is simply exhilarating. I have not been so much moved for a long time. He is a real mystic of an odd kind.'[1]

---

[1] Fr. C.C. Martindale, *The Life of Monsignor Robert Hugh Benson,* Vol. 2, p. 90.

(And this precious tidbit unrelated to my topic: "During these visits [of Benson's] to America he was assiduous in visiting theatres. Especially Mr. Chesterton's Magic fascinated him; he was constantly behind the scenes at its rehearsals."[2])

Father C.C. Martindale says that in late December, 1905, a certain Mr. Frederick Rolfe, author of *Hadrian VII*, drew Father Benson's attention to Saint Simon, the author of French socialism. Benson wrote to his mother in December of 1905:

> Yes, Russia is ghastly. Which reminds me that I have an idea for a book so vast and tremendous that I daren't think about it. Have you ever heard of Saint Simon? Well, mix up Saint Simon, Russia breaking loose, Napoleon, Evan Roberts, the Pope, and Antichrist; and see if any idea suggests itself. But I'm afraid it is too big. I should like to form a syndicate on it, but that is an idea, I have no doubt at all.[3]

To Mr. Rolfe himself he writes on January 19, 1906: "Antichrist is beginning to obsess me. If it is ever written, it will be a BOOK. Do you know about the Freemasons? Socialism? I am going to avoid scientific developments, and confine myself to social... Oh! If I dare to write all that I think! In any case it will take years."[4]

It didn't take years. *The Lord of the World* came out (as mentioned) in 1907. Thus Chesterton and Benson were writing around the same time. Perhaps future research will uncover whether or not there was any mutual influence. However, they were both deeply immersed into "what the Spirit was saying to the churches" of their era. This is what I find fascinating, that

---

[2] *Ibid.*, p. 176.

[3] *Ibid.*, pp. 65-66.

[4] *Ibid.*, p. 66.

all three writers portray very similar—at times identical—characteristics about the spirit of the Antichrist, and about the lies perpetrated by the father of lies.

As we have seen, Chesterton does not speak of the Antichrist but of Lucifer. Chesterton's scenario is limited to England, and his scope is not as vast, nor as explicitly and consciously cosmic and apocalyptic, as Soloviov's and Benson's. But I believe he was describing the same ultimate conflict.

Faithful to the tradition of the Fathers, it was Newman's belief that the Antichrist would be a *definite individual*:

> Let no man deceive you by any means, 'he [St. Paul] says, for that Day shall not come, except there comes a falling away first, and except first that man of sin be revealed, the son of perdition.' As long as the world lasts, this passage of Scripture will be full of reverent interest to Christians. It is their duty ever to be watching for the advent of their Lord, to search for the signs of it in all that happens around them; and above all to keep in mind this great and awful sign of which St. Paul speaks to the Thessalonians. As our Lord's first coming had its forerunner, so will the second have its own. The first was 'One more than a prophet,' the Holy Baptist: the second will be more than an enemy of Christ; it will be the very image of Satan, the fearful and hateful Antichrist.[5]

Chesterton portrays Satan/Antichrist as fostering a variety of attitudes which deny Christ and gospel values; I've outlined a few of them. In the last days there will be a tsunami of lies: "Dear children, this is the last hour; and as you have heard that the Antichrist is coming, even now many Antichrists have come. Who is the liar? It is the man who denies that

[5] Newman, pp. 44-45.

Jesus is the Christ. Such a man is the Antichrist—he denies the Father and the Son."[6]

DIES IRAE

This is the title of Chesterton's last chapter in *B&C*. It corresponds, in a general way, to the scriptural vision of Revelation 20: Satan will be let loose for a while and do immense harm; fire comes down from heaven and consumes him; Christ will then come to establish a new heaven and a new earth: "Satan will be released from his prison and will go out to deceive the nations. (Rev. 7) But fire came down from heaven. (Rev. 9) Then I saw a great white throne and him who was seated on it." (Rev. 11)

Soloviov's and Benson's final visions are more grandiose, Chesterton's more humble—a mere insane asylum burning to the ground with all the sane people escaping. But he certainly has ultimate visions in mind; even the language is there. As all the characters come together for the final scene, MacIan says to Turnbull:

> 'There are two states where one meets so many old friends. One is a dream, the other is the end of the world. I say this is not a dream.' 'You really mean to suggest –' began Turnbull. 'Be silent! or I shall say it all wrong. It's hard to explain, anyhow. An apocalypse is the opposite of a dream. A dream is falser than the outer life. But the end of the world is more actual than the world it ends. I don't say this is really the end of the world, but it's something like that—it's the end of something. All the people are crowding to a point.'

In a variety of ways Chesterton emphasizes in his writings

[6] 1 John 2:18-22.

that the Church is less mad than the world; Christians should admit and realize that sometimes they have participated in the world's madness; but the Prince of this World, the "Lord of the World," will ultimately be defeated by Christ present in the Church.

Pope Sylvester, in Benson's novel, thinks the same:

> But the centre of his position was simple faith. The Catholic Religion, he knew well enough, gave the only adequate explanation of the universe; it did not unlock all mysteries, but it unlocked more than any other key known to man. He saw well enough that the failure of Christianity to unite all men one to another rested not upon its feebleness but its strength; its lines met in eternity, not in time.[7]

Chesterton does not have one "Lord of the World" incarnating the Antichrist, as Julian Felsenburgh in Benson's novel. ("Lord of the World" is also one of the Antichrist's titles in Soloviov). Nor is Chesterton's scenario *the* end of the world. But it will be one stage. At some point Christ in his Church will be victorious over the "isms" (antichrists) that seek to stabilize the world without God as the center.

And then the purifying flames. Old Mr. Durand sets fire to the building "in accordance with the strict principles of the social contract." MacIan cries, again, in apocalyptic language, "Now is the judgment of this world." There are all sorts of confusions with the resolution of this and that theme. One of the most striking and happy resolutions is that of our atheist friend Turnbull who escapes the fire by leaning on both the "strong shoulder" of the beautiful Madeleine and that of the duelist-become-friend MacIan.

---

[7] Benson, p. 263.

The fire, though it had dropped in one or two places, was, upon the whole, higher and more unquenchable than ever. The tall and steady forest of fire must have been already a portent visible to the whole circle of land and sea. That forest of fire wavered, and was cloven in the centre. One half of the huge fire sloped one way toward the inland heights, the other half sloped out eastward toward the sea. Down the centre of this trough, or chasm, a little path ran, cleared of all but ashes, and down this little path was walking a little old man singing as if he were alone in a wood of spring. As the little singing figure came nearer and nearer, Evan fell on his knees, and after an instant Madeleine fell on her knees, and after a longer instant Turnbull followed. Then the little old man went past them singing down that corridor of flames.

The good guys escape the flames; the bad guys fall in; Professor Lucifer, instead of falling into the "sea of sulfur," flies off in his spaceship (perhaps indicating that this is not Chesterton's vision of the final end of the world but, as he said, the end of something.) The final reflection is given to MacIan: "He looked vaguely about at the fire that was already fading, and there among the ashes laid two shining things that had survived the fire, his sword and Turnbull's, fallen haphazard in the pattern of a cross."

A penultimate stage—"the end of something"—towards the end of the world will be, in Chesterton's view, the triumph of the foolishness of the cross over the circular, balled-up logic of the rationalists.[8]

Benson's "Victory"

I read Benson's final Chapter, "The Victory," several times, but I still couldn't figure out exactly how he was ending the end of

[8] Cf. I Cor. 1:18-25.

the world! It seems I was not alone. For many other people at the time of *The Lord of the World*'s publication were also unclear as well as to just how he finished off the world. I suspect that Benson himself was not sure! He wrote: "I have finished ANTICHRIST. And really there is no more to be said. It just settles things. Of course I am nervous about the last chapter—it is what one may call perhaps just a trifle ambitious to describe the End of the World. (No!) But it has been done."[9]

It ends like this: A Cardinal betrays the Pope's whereabouts. Julian Felsenburgh and his cohorts fly off in their volors (airships) to bomb Peter II in Nazareth. The Pope prepares with several hours of adoration before the Blessed Sacrament, celebrates a Mass of Pentecost, and conducts a procession outside with the monstrance with "the Whiteness of God made Man." The *Tantum Ergo* is sung and its phrases interspersed with descriptions of what is happening.

There are suggestions of the heavenly hosts being present: "Then, with a roar, came the thunder again, pealing in circle beyond circle of those tremendous Presences—Thrones and Powers."[10] Felsenburgh, the Antichrist, is coming: "He was coming now, swifter than ever, the heir of temporal ages and the Exile of eternity, the final piteous Prince of rebels." There is the final phrase of the Benediction hymn repeated twice—*Procedenti ab utroque, compar sit laudatio*—and then the final sentence: "Then this world passed, and the glory of it. The End."

Really, it isn't clear how Benson's apocalypse ends the world. People interpreted Benson's final cataclysm according to their preferences: some socialists were delighted that the Church had been destroyed; some people sympathetic to the Church

---

[9] *Ibid.*, p. 74.

[10] *Ibid.*, pp. 351-352.

originally thought an enemy had written the book; others lost hope in the Church. Father Martindale admits the book occasioned "sheer bewilderment" on the part of many.

But if the ending was unclear, the main message of the book was not. Besides its anti-modernist intent, "Benson pictures humanity consciously refusing the higher kind of life which the Church proclaims to it. This rejection of the Supernatural is incarnated in Julian Felsenburgh, who says, 'I, in my completed human evolution, am enough.' To him Christianity answers, 'You are not.'"[11] It is in this theme of "kneeling before the world," as Jacques Maritain once expressed it, where *B&C* and *LW* converge.

THE END OF THE WORLD ACCORDING TO SOLOVIOV

After the Emperor offers his proposals in the above-mentioned Congress for the Unification of All Cults, he finally asks: "Tell me yourselves, Christians, what is it that you value most in Christianity?"[12] Elder John, representing Orthodoxy, answered quietly: 'Great sovereign! What we value most in Christianity is Christ himself—in his person. All comes from him, for we know that in him dwells all the fullness of the Godhead bodily. Confess his name, and we will accept you with love as the true forerunner of his second glorious coming.'

The Emperor is livid with rage. Elder John shouts, "Little children, it is Antichrist!" He is struck dead by magical power. Pope Peter II also rises up, not quietly but with "a word, loud and distinct: '*Contradicitur*! Our only Lord is Jesus Christ, the Son of the living God.'"

He too is struck dead. Professor Pauli and a remnant retire into the desert. Several days later they return, bringing the bodies

---

[11] Martindale, II, p. 82.

[12] Soloviov, 184. Quotes in this section are from this text unless otherwise noted.

of Peter and John with them. They miraculously come back to life. An army of Jews, also deceived by the Emperor's offer to give them domination over the whole world, rebel.

The armies come together around the Dead Sea, where a volcano arises. "Streams of fire flowed together into a flaming lake that swallowed up the Emperor himself, together with his numberless forces." Soloviov's ending is worth quoting in full:

> Meanwhile, the Jews hastened to Jerusalem in fear and trembling, calling for salvation to the God of Israel. When the Holy City was already in sight, the heavens were rent by vivid lightning from the east to the west, and they saw Christ coming toward them in royal apparel and with the wounds from the nails in his outstretched hands. At the same time, the company of Christians led by Peter, John, and Paul came from Sinai to Zion, and from various other parts hurried more triumphant multitudes, consisting of all the Jews and Christians who had been killed by the Antichrist. For a thousand years, they lived and reigned with Christ.
>
> Here Father Pansophius wished to end his narrative, which had for its object not a universal cataclysm of creation but the conclusion of our historical process which consists in the appearance, glorification, and destruction of the Antichrist.

Soloviov's end of the world narrative is much more scriptural than the other two novels. There is a woman crowned with twelve stars who leads the remnant into the desert. The Antichrist is destroyed, Christ returns, and reigns with his faithful for a thousand years.

I think Soloviov's Antichrist is the most powerful of the three stories we have been considering, but Chesterton's contains many more penetrating insights into the deceits of Satan.

My contention is that Chesterton's *B&C* deserves to be

placed with Soloviov's and Benson's "more serious" stories of the Antichrist at the turn of the century. It may be another instance of Chesterton's insights not being taken seriously because of the lightness and humor of his style. John Coates writes: "*The Ball and the Cross* (1910) belongs to a genre which has probably never been adequately examined or assessed, a genre not generally accepted as 'art' in its own time and a leading casualty of subsequent critical fashions and orthodoxies. The genre might be variously labeled a 'Philosophical novel,' 'novel of ideas,' even 'religious novel.'"[13]

Coates goes on to quote many reviewers as to how unacceptable *B&C* was according to the contemporary canons of literature: "'It is indeed,' as Robert Lynd put it in *The Daily News*, 'not so much a novel as a phantasmagoria.'"[14] Could this unacceptability from a literary point of view have obscured the serious value of it as a genuine story of the spirit of the Antichrist?

Gardner, as I have noted, says the novel can be read on several levels. But perhaps too many people only read it on the level he describes at the end of his article: "On the other hand, one may still enjoy reading it for its colourful style, with its constant alliteration, amusing puns, and clever paradoxes; for its purple passages about sunsets, dawns, and silver moonlight; and for the humour and melodrama of its crazy plot."[15] But I believe that when we put *B&C* in the context of the turn of century, and compare it with other literary expressions of the spirit of the Antichrist, it achieves its proper and prophetic place: It is one of Chesterton's best literary testimonies to his life-long "battle with the father of lies."

---

[13] John Coates, "*The Ball and the Cross* and the Edwardian Novel of Ideas," *The Chesterton Review*, Vol. XVIII, No. 1, February, 1992, p. 49.

[14] *Ibid.*, p. 49.

[15] Gardner, p. 47. I think it's very unfortunate that these literary niceties are all Gardiner can recommend about *B&C*!

The Fearful and Hateful Antichrist of Benson and Soloviov

Soloviov and Benson paint the story of the Antichrist in broad and obvious strokes; and Benson elaborates the plot and subplots. But for sheer insight into the spirit of the Antichrist, and how he tries to deceive men's minds, Chesterton has the more subtle and copious perceptions. In his *Autobiography* he summed up its purpose thus: "I believe that the suggestion that the modern world is organised in relation to the most obvious and urgent of all questions, not so much to answer it wrongly, as to prevent it being answered at all, is a social suggestion that really has a great deal in it."[16]

The fact that Chesterton himself did not particularly *like* this novel may also have helped to downplay its importance. In a copy of *The Ball and Cross* owned by Fr. John O'Connor, Chesterton inscribed a poem:

> This is a book I do not like,
> Take it away to Heckmondwike,
> A lurid exile, lost and sad,
> To punish it for being bad.
> You need not take it from the shelf
> (I tried to read it once myself:
> The speeches jerk, the chapters sprawl,
> The story makes no sense at all)
> Hide it your Yorkshire moors among
> Where no man speaks the English tongue.[17]

But the verses end on a more hopeful note: "Take then this book I do not like—It may improve in Heckmondwike."

Surely these disparaging comments refer to the literary canons of the novel and not to its ideas, which are very profound.

---

[16] Quoted by Gardner, p. 46.

[17] Ian Ker, *G.K. Chesterton, A Biography* (Oxford University Press: Oxford, 2011), p. 265.

William Oddie points out several times that Chesterton's disparaging remarks about his own writings should not be taken too seriously; and too often they have influenced the opinions of other critics.[18]

Chesterton and Newman

There is one final question: Was Chesterton influenced by Newman's writings on the Antichrist? Before I attempt an answer, let us listen again to Newman. It may then be easier to give an answer to the question. I offer it also as a good meditation on watchfulness for Christians of all eras of history:

> I have two remarks to add: first that it is quite certain, that if such a persecution has been foretold, it has not yet come, and therefore is to come. We may be wrong in thinking that Scripture foretells it, though it has been the common belief, I may say, of all ages; but if there be a persecution, it is still future. So that every generation of Christians should be on the watch-tower, looking out—nay, more and more, as time goes on.[19]
>
> Next, I observe that signs do occur from time to time, not to enable us to fix the day, for that is forbidden, but to show us it is coming. The world grows old—the earth is crumbling away—the night is far spent—the day is at hand. The shadows begin to move—the old forms of empire, which have lasted ever since our Lord was with us, heave and tremble before our eyes, and nod to their fall. These it is that keep Him from us—He is behind them. When they go, Antichrist will be released from 'that which upholdeth,' and after his short but fearful season, Christ will come.

---

[18] Oddie in *Romance* quotes from Maisie Ward: *A Handful of Authors:* ed. Dorothy Collins (Sheed and Ward: New York, 1953). p. 342.

[19] Newman, pp. 102-106.

After all, it may not be a persecution of blood and death, but of craft and subtlety only—not of miracles, but of natural wonders and powers of human skill, human acquirements in the hands of the devil. Satan may adopt the more alarming weapons of deceit—he may hide himself—he may attempt to seduce us in little things, and so to move the Church, not all at once, but by little and little from her true position. It is his policy to split us up and divide us, to dislodge us gradually from off our rock of strength.

Such meditations as these may be turned to good account. It will act as a curb upon our self-willed, selfish hearts, to believe that a persecution is in store for the Church, whether or not it comes in our days. Surely, with this prospect before us, we cannot bear to give ourselves up to thoughts of ease and comfort, of making money, settling well, or rising in the world. Surely, with this prospect before us, we cannot but feel that we are, what all Christians really are in the best estate (nay, rather would wish to be, had they their will, if they be Christians in heart), pilgrims, watchers waiting for the morning, waiting for the light, eagerly straining our eyes for the first dawn of day—looking out for the Lord's coming, His glorious advent, when He will end the reign of sin and wickedness, accomplish the number of His elect, and perfect those who at present struggle with infirmity; yet in their hearts love and obey him.[20]

"Satan may adopt the more alarming weapons of deceit—he may hide himself—he may attempt to seduce us in little things, and so to move the Church, not all at once, but by little and little from her true position." Is not *B&C* a very explicit and detailed exposition of this profound insight of Blessed John

[20] Newman, pp. 102-106.

Henry Newman?

It is common knowledge that Chesterton had read Newman: "Chesterton's claim to have generated his arguments in a literary vacuum, however, is perhaps disingenuous. Asked to draw up a 'scheme of reading' for 1908, he suggested Butler's *Analogy*, Coleridge's *Confessions of an Inquiring Spirit*, Newman's *Apology*, St. Augustine's *Confessions*, and the *Summa Theologica* of St. Thomas Aquinas."[21] Also, in *Handful*, Chesterton has an article "The Style of Newman," and also mentions Newman's *Apologia*. Chesterton mentions Newman's first lecture on "The Position of English Catholics." This means that he was familiar with, and had access to, Newman's early works.

At the very time he is writing *B&C*, in a letter to the editor of *The Nation*, someone asks, "Has Mr. Chesterton ever heard of Newman?" Chesterton responds: "You also ask me whether I have ever 'heard of Newman.' I seem to know the name. In fact, I have an impression (erroneous no doubt) that I have read most of his books."[22] It is very probable, then, that he had read Newman's "The Patristical Idea of Antichrist" which appeared as *Tracts for the Times*, No. 83, 1838.

It may be of interest that Newman also wrote several articles, even before his conversion, refuting the notion that the Pope of Rome is the Antichrist. "The only question is this, 'Has Christ, or has He not, appointed a body representative of Him on earth during His absence?' If He has, the Pope is not Antichrist; if He has not, every bishop in England is Antichrist."[23] "If we have been defending it, this has been from no love, let our readers

---

[21] Oddie, *Romance of Orthodoxy*.

[22] "Modernism," p. 15.

[23] *Essays Critical and Historical,* Vol. II (London: Longmans, Green, and Co., New York, 1887), p. 112-185. Quotes in this paragraph are from this essay.

be assured, of the Roman party among us at this day [1840]." The passages about the Antichrist in scripture "cannot by any sober mind be applied to the ecclesiastical events or persons of the past ages of Christianity." In *The Everlasting Man* Chesterton says that if the Pope is not the Vicar of Christ then he certainly is the Antichrist. Was this remark inspired by Newman?

THE DARKNESS OF THE BRAIN OF MAN

I submit that in his closing remarks from *The New Jerusalem*[24] we have one of the most important keys to Chesterton's life and writings, and a succinct statement of the thesis of this book. In a few paragraphs he mentions the mind, fairy-tales, theology, and drama—all areas to which he applied his great mind. And if battle is an all-pervasive theme in his writings, in his own mind *it is a battle with this "unfathomable evil at our very feet"* which he here relates to all four areas:

> [realm of the mind] In all our brains, certainly in mine, were buried things as bad as any buried under that bitter sea [he is referring to the demons (Matt 8: 30-32) who begged to be sent into a herd of pigs. "The whole herd rushed down the steep bank into the lake and died in the water."]; and if He did not come to do battle with them, even in the darkness of the brain of man, I know not why He came. Certainly it was not only to talk about flowers or to talk about Socialism.

> [fairy tales] The more truly we can see life as a fairy-tale, the more clearly the tale resolves itself into war with the dragon that is wasting the fairyland.

> [theology] I remember distinguished men among liberal theologians, who found it more difficult to believe in one than

[24] *The New Jerusalem*, p. 275.

in many. They admitted in the New Testament an attestation to evil spirits, but not to a general enemy of mankind.

[drama] As some are said to want the drama of Hamlet without the Prince of Denmark, they would have the drama of Hell without the Prince of Darkness.

A very important aspect of Chesterton's prophetic and apologetic mission was keeping alive belief in the reality of evil spirits. While not the most cheery part of his legacy, it is an essential dimension of the truth of the gospel. And it is a testimony to his greatness that he did not shirk from the more difficult truths of the Christian faith.

Despite a deep personal belief in these truths, he was able to maintain his celebrated and often over-emphasized joy, mirth, playfulness, and wonder. It is right that he should be known mostly for these latter exuberant traits. At the Last Supper the Lord prayed both that we would be protected from the evil one,[25] *and that our joy would be complete.*[26] Emphasizing this *joy dimension* of his prophetic message is how I'd like to end this very serious chapter on the Antichrist.

In *The Return of Don Quixote*, Olive Ashley explains to her friend and host, Rosamund Severne: "You must think me mad to be talking so when you suffer; but it's as if I were bursting with news—with something bigger than all the universe of sorrow. Rosamund, *there really is joy*. Not rejoicing, but joy; not rejoicing at this or that; *but the thing* itself we only see reflected in mirrors—which sometimes break."[27]

---

[25] John 17:15.

[26] John 15:24.

[27] Quoted by Knight, p. 77.

CHAPTER SIX

GEORGE MACDONALD, EVIL, AND THE DEVIL

In Chapter Twelve of *The Tumbler of God* I treated briefly Chesterton's relationship with the writings and person of George MacDonald. I want to do something similar here. I've already mentioned that Chesterton said MacDonald's *The Princess and the Goblin* was very significant in his life. Here is his statement, written in the Introduction he wrote for Greville MacDonald's biography of his father, George:

> But in a certain rather special sense I for one can really testify to a book that has made a difference to my whole existence, which helped me to see things in a certain way from the start; a vision of things which even so real a revolution as a change of religious allegiance has substantially only crowned and confirmed. Of all the stories I ever read… it remains the most real, the most realistic, in the exact sense of the phrase the most like life. It is called *The Princess and the Goblin*, and is by George MacDonald…[1]

Oddie comments about this statement: "Any book thus described has to be given more than passing attention by anyone seeking to trace the growth of Chesterton's imaginative and intellectual life."[2]

What has particularly led me to include this Chapter on MacDonald is what Chesterton said was a very profound truth he found in *The Princess*:

---

[1] In *G.K.C. as M.C.*: ed. J.P. de Fonseka, pp. 163-64.
[2] Oddie, p. 34.

I am speaking of what may emphatically be called the presence of household gods—and household goblins. And the picture of life in this parable is not only truer than the image of a journey like that of the Pilgrim's Progress; it is even truer than the mere image of a siege like that of the Holy War. There is something not only imaginative but intimately true about the idea of the goblins being below the house and capable of besieging it from the cellars. When the evil things besieging us do appear, they do not appear outside but inside.[3]

For Chesterton, the main source of evil is in the "darkness of the brain." The goblins *under the house* where the Princess lived struck Chesterton as particularly true about the human condition. Since this story was so influential in Chesterton's life and thinking, I wondered how and if MacDonald's view of evil and the devil might have become part of Chesterton's outlook as well.

It is commonly recognized that because Chesterton was such a creative writer it is difficult to show the direct influence of others on his writings. Thus, this chapter is simply meant to provide another general background to Chesterton's understanding of the devil. I will present some of MacDonald's thinking about evil and the devil, indicate a few possible connections with Chesterton's views, and then leave it up to the reader to make any further conclusions concerning the interrelationship of their ideas. In a brief reading of some of MacDonald's work with my eye on the devil, I believe I saw some similarities between the two writers; but that is as far as I will hazard any direct influence.

This chapter is also a way—as I expressed in *The Tumbler*—of paying tribute to a man whom Chesterton admired and who probably was more influential in his own vision of reality than we can document with any certainty.

---

[3] Oddie, p. 37.

For my purposes I chose three literary works of MacDonald to illustrate three sources of evil: the evil tendency of the personal will (*Lilith*); the goblins as the source of evil in the human heart (*The Princess and the Goblin*); and MacDonald's direct treatment of the devil in his sermon "The Temptation in the Wilderness" in *Unspoken Sermons*.[4] We definitely know that Chesterton read *The Princess*, so I will give a brief treatment of who the goblins might represent. He also mentions two of MacDonald's novels that he read—*Phantastes* and *Lilith*.[5] *Lilith* was MacDonald's last major work, and which his son Greville considered his father's masterpiece. (His mother didn't like it!) It expresses some of MacDonald's mature ideas, especially about the nature of evil, which is my main concern.

Did Chesterton ever read some of MacDonald's *Unspoken Sermons*? I don't know. But "The Temptation in the Wilderness" will be considered here as it contains some significant notions of MacDonald's understanding of Satan. Quite simply, because MacDonald had a significant influence on Chesterton, it seemed appropriate to explore briefly his views concerning evil and Satan as possibly influencing some of Chesterton's ideas.

Riddled with Evil

As I've used Mark Knight's book *Chesterton and Evil* as a sort of background to my treatment of Chesterton on that topic, so I will be using a rather lengthy article as a background for my study of MacDonald's understanding of evil in relation to

---

[4] George MacDonald, *Unspoken Sermons, Series I, II, and III* (Wilder Publications, LLC: Radford, VA, 2008). "The Temptation in the Wilderness," pp. 50-63. All quotations in this section are from this book unless otherwise noted.

[5] Daniel Gabelman, "Nocturnal Anarchist, Mystic, and Fairytale King: G.K. Chesterton's Portrait of George MacDonald, *VII, An Anglo-American Literary Review*, Vol. 28, 2011. Published by the Marion E. Wade Center of Wheaton College, pp. 27-46.

Chesterton. It is entitled *Riddled with Evil: Fantasy as Theodicy in George MacDonald's Phantastes and Lilith*, by Courtney Salvey.[6] And since Chesterton called MacDonald a mystic, I will also be using Charles Beaucham's *Lilith and Mysticism*.[7] He tries to demonstrate that MacDonald was a mystic according to some definitions of that phenomenon. (This was also my approach in seeking to demonstrate Chesterton's mysticism—that it corresponds to *some* definitions of mysticism.)

In recently discovered early writings of Chesterton on MacDonald entitled, "George MacDonald, The Mystic," Chesterton defines a mystic as "one who sees round every object a halo from the hidden sun."[8] He concludes: "The nineteenth century is a century of steam, of machinery, of board schools, of dock strikes, of journalism: but it is with all and above all, an age of mysticism. The agnostic is the antithesis of the mystic, but he is also his forerunner. Until religion ceases to be an arbitrary science it cannot establish its claim as a language beyond the scientific. Mystics abound in this century and of them, Dr. George MacDonald, is the most remarkable." (I wish I had known about these early texts of Chesterton for my book *The Tumbler of God*! I would have included Chesterton as one of the mystics who "abound in this century.")

So I wish to suggest, therefore, that MacDonald's intuitions about evil, especially in *Lilith*, were the fruit of his *mysticism*. Beaucham quotes Greville as saying that his father, in writing *Lilith*, "was possessed of a feeling that it was a mandate direct from God, for which he himself was to find form and clothing.

---

[6] http://www.snc.edu/northwind/documents/By_volume/sk004_Volume_27_(2008)/sk002_Riddled_with_Evil=_Fantasy_as_Theodicy_in_George_MacDonald's_Phantastes_and_Lilith_-_Courtney_Salvey.pdf.

[7] Charles Beaucham, *North Wind* Vol. 28 (2009), pp. 13-32.

[8] Gabelman, pp. 42-44.

Its first writing is unlike anything he ever did."[9]

It would be logical to begin with *The Princess* since this tale was so significant for Chesterton, and we have his comments about its influence. But, first, I will give a general background to MacDonald's whole understanding of evil, concentrating on *Lilith*. It will give a good context to an understanding of the goblins in *The Princess*. With these two works which deal indirectly with Satan, I will then conclude with MacDonald's more explicit treatment of the devil in his sermon, "The Temptation in the Wilderness."

I am not concerned in any way with the literary characteristics of MacDonald's imaginative mind. I am not competent in this area; and besides, much of it is already available. My concern is to flesh out, in a very rudimentary and limited way, his understanding of the devil, and relate it to the subject of my book. It will be suggestive rather than seeking to document any definite connections with Chesterton. I offer it merely as a possible influence of MacDonald on Chesterton's understanding of the Enemy.

The following insights are from Salvey.

MacDonald is not a Platonist. He does not locate the source of evil in the material world. MacDonald's fantasies reveal an Augustinian concept of the universe: evil is the privation of good, and all things with substance are good. The main source of evil is the will of the self. MacDonald himself wrote: "The highest in man is neither his intellect nor his imagination nor his reason; all are inferior to his will, and indeed, in a grand way, dependent upon it: his will must meet God's—a will *distinct* from God's, else were no *harmony* possible between them. Not the less, therefore, but the more, is all God's. For God creates

---

[9] Beaucham, p. 18.

in man the power to will His will. It may cost God a suffering man can never know, to bring the man to the point at which he wills His will."[10] Evil is the non-substantive privation of good. Everything that God made is good. Evil has no substance otherwise it would be good. Evil is the loss of good.

MacDonald believed in the goodness of all creation. Whence, then, evil? MacDonald followed Augustine in the *Confessions*, "…defecting from that which supremely is, to that which has less of being—this is to begin to have an evil will." What we seek is not evil in itself, but what is wicked in the inordinate desire. There is no evil force in the universe [in the Manichean sense.] Augustine conceived the devil and his fallen angels as individual examples of the entrance of evil into an individual existence.

Salvey devotes half of his article to *Phantastes*, and half to *Lilith*. I am most interested in *Lilith*, but this comment about *Phantastes* relates to MacDonald's general presentation of evil. (It is not necessary to know the story line of this fable for this brief selection):

> *Phantastes* illustrates that evil is not within the natural world but corrupts it, a parasite on anything with substance, including the psyche. While evil characters scurry through fantastic landscape, MacDonald never presents the Devil as the ultimate source of all evil. Evil has no single source in the universe from which it emanates (which would be a reverse source of the good.) Instead, MacDonald presents evil as a shadow over the self, locating evil within the self. The shadow in each definition is something sinister, something evil: it is a negation of good.

---

[10] George MacDonald, *Hope of the Gospel* (Bibliobazaar: Charleston, SC, 2007), p. 15.

Lilith

It will be necessary to offer a few general details of the story of *Lilith* in order to understand MacDonald's treatment of evil in what is considered his masterpiece.

Mr. Vane, the protagonist, passes through a mirror into a region of seven dimensions. (This was the inspiration for the children entering into Narnia through the wardrobe of Lewis.) He comes across a house of beds where people sleep until the end of the world. Continuing on, he meets the Little Ones, children who never grow up. They either remain pure, or become selfish, turning into "bags" or bad giants. After conversing with Lona, the eldest of the children, Vane decides to help the children. But the Raven (Adam) tells him that he needs to sleep with the dreamers who are sleeping before he can help the bags.

Continuing on his journey he meets Lilith, Adam's first wife, and the princess of Bulika. Vane, although nearly blinded by Lilith's beauty, eventually leads the Little Ones in a battle against Bulika. Lona, Vane's love, turns out to be Lilith's daughter, and is killed by her own mother. Lilith, however, is captured and brought to Adam and Eve at the house of death, where they struggle to make her open her hand, fused shut, in which she holds the water the Little Ones need to grow. Only when she gives it up can Lilith join the sleepers in blissful dreams, free of sin. After a long struggle, Lilith bids Adam cut her hand from her body; it is done. Lilith sleeps, and Vane is sent to bury the hand; water flows from the hole and washes over the land. Vane is then allowed to join the Little Ones, already asleep, in their dreaming. He takes his bed, next to Lona's, and finds true life in death.[11]

"Lilith contains MacDonald's clearer theodicy, his explanation of evil in the universe." There is a Great Shadow (the Devil) in

---

[11] My summary from George MacDonald, *Lilith, A Romance* (Merchant Books, 2009).

the story. Yet the responsibility for evil and sin in the world is not this Shadow but always the choices of the self. MacDonald is not a dualist. The self of the ego is the source of evil in Lilith. MacDonald enters deeply into the exploration of the nature of evil through the consideration of a fallen angel, Lilith. (Lilith's nature is not clear in the story. Sometimes she is human (Adam's first wife), sometimes she is a fallen angel.) Lilith ensnares the heart of the great Shadow and he becomes her slave.

There are a variety of interpretations about who or what Lilith represents. In 1933 C.S. Lewis wrote in a letter to his friend Arthur Greeves his reflections on *Lilith*: "Lilith is still quite beyond me."[12] He meant the meaning of Lilith. But then he continued with a tentative explanation: "One can trace in her specially the Will to Power—which here fits in quite well—but there is a great deal more than that. She is also the real ideal somehow spoiled; she is not primarily a sexual symbol, but includes the characteristic female abuse of sex, which is the love of Power." Further on Lewis writes: "[Vane] finds himself the *jailer* of Lilith: i.e., he is now living in the state of tension with the evil thing inside him only just held down, and at a terrible cost—until he (or Lilith—the Lilith part of him) at last repents."

Then he closes the letter with this remark about the Lovers (the good guys) and the Bags (the bad guys): "I have emphasized the eternal side too much. Correct everything above by remembering that it is not only the Lovers outside against the Bags, but equally the Lover in himself against the Bag in himself." One interpretation of the story of *Lilith* is that it is a description of MacDonald's inner life. And Lewis, in the above quotes, alludes to this interpretation. It is the one I will be following, for I want

---

[12] Quoted by Stephen Prickett, "George MacDonald and the European Literary Tradition," *The Chesterton Review*, Vol. XXIII, Nos. 1 & 2, February/May 2001, Seton Hall University, South Orange, New Jersey, p. 86.

to make a case for *Lilith being the evil will to power within us all, the evil will to resist goodness*, love, God. MacDonald located evil principally in the self. *Lilith* is his final imaginative expression of this source of evil in the world.

Universalism

Many years ago I read *Lilith*, and the only thing I always remembered about it was the frightening description of this unimaginable power of *Lilith* to resist grace, repentance, real life, love. I will reproduce some of the relevant passages below, but first, a word of what preceded my study of *Lilith* for this book.

A few months before starting work on this chapter I was engaged in a study of Christian Universalism, the belief that everyone—and for some universalists this means the devils also– will ultimately be saved. MacDonald, as is well-known, was a universalist, although he never used that term. One of the most convincing arguments for universalism concerns the philosophical view that no created will can resist forever the overwhelming love of God.

I began the study for this chapter, therefore, with some reading about Universalism. *Lilith* immediately struck me as MacDonald's frightening description of the hideous power we all have to resist the love of God. But not forever! *Lilith*, as has been mentioned, is one of MacDonald's last major works. My theory is that, in *Lilith*, MacDonald has portrayed a selfish will of demonic proportions, and then gave one of the most profound literary descriptions of how even such an obstinate will must eventually be conquered by Love. My opinion is that MacDonald uses *Lilith* as a universalist argument against the possibility of everlasting resistance to the love of God.

As noted, I have been using Prof. Stephen Prickett's article in my study of MacDonald. I asked him, in a private correspondence, if he thought *Lilith* could be MacDonald's argument for this universalist position. He wrote: "In a word, yes. I think you are absolutely right about Lilith as an argument for universalism. I agree entirely with your argument."

Before quoting MacDonald's imaginative way of supporting this philosophical argument for universalism, let me quote, from the universalist literature, a more ethical and humane expression of the same argument that I find in *Lilith*. It is by John A.T. Robinson of *Honest to God* fame in his book *In the End, God*:

> We have known what it is to be confronted by a love too strong to resist. We had no intention of yielding one whit of our proud independence. And yet we fell: it was too much for us. It forced us to a free acknowledgment of its power. And how wonderful that moment of surrender was!
>
> And then we seemed to hear a voice, which told us we need have no fear at all. It spoke of another love, which, though we knew it not, had all the while been meeting us in that love we knew. It was this love that had really been drawing us to itself, and imparting to us the sense of return to our home. And we laughed that we had ever allowed ourselves to think that there might not be a power without us great enough to conquer those last shreds of our pride and independence. For we knew that the power of this love could experience no bounds at all. Sooner or later, as we let it, it would bring us back to the haven where we would be. We rejoiced to know that we could not stop it.[13]

MacDonald recounts the origin, identity, and sin of *Lilith*: "He brought me (Adam) an angelic splendor to be my wife: there she lies! For her first thought was power; she counted it

---

[13] John A. T. Robinson, *In the End, God* (Cascade Books: Eugene, Oregon, 2011), p. 136.

slavery to be one with me, and bear children for Him who gave her being. Finding, however, that I would but love and honour, never obey and worship her, she poured out her blood to escape me, fled to the army of the aliens and soon had so ensnared the heart of the great Shadow that he became her slave, wrought her will, and made her queen."[14] So, here, *Lilith* is Adam's first wife who is too proud to obey the laws of her nature implanted in her by the Creator.

I am going to present now one of the most penetrating and "diabolically frightening" accounts of resistance to goodness in any literature that I have ever read. My theory is that it is not only an account of human resistance to goodness, but is MacDonald's portrayal of *the resistance of evil spirits as well*. He believed that even they would ultimately have to succumb to the onslaught of Love.

Why his account strikes me as so unique is because I have never read, in our Christian theology, any very penetrating or profound insights into the resistance of the devils, the perverted rationale behind their motivation. We say, simply, that they would not obey; or that they set themselves up as gods; or they were too proud to submit to a Power greater than themselves, and so forth. But what I believe we have in the following dialogue is MacDonald's dramatic presentation of a resistance that is almost unbelievably uncompromising, something of what the resistance of demons must be like. It was his way of teaching that no created will—not even those of fallen angelic beings—can forever resist divine Love.

Listen to the depth of this resistance as attributed to Lilith.

Mara, the *Sorrowful Mother*, is pleading for her submission. (Was MacDonald, the Protestant, sneaking in a reference to the

---

[14] *Lilith* (Merchant Books, 2009). The following quotes are from this book unless otherwise noted.

Blessed Virgin Mary? Was it the intercession of Mary that finally won Lilith over?) This dialogue can serve, as well, as a meditation for all of us, describing our own power of resistance to grace.

"Repent, and be again an angel of God." "Will you not be your real self?" "I will not," she said. "I will be myself and not another." "Alas, you are another now, not yourself! Will you not be your real self?" "I will be what I mean myself now." "If you were restored, you could make amends for the misery you have caused?" "I would do after my nature." "You do not know it; your nature is good, and you do evil!" "I will do as my Self pleases—as my Self desires." "You do as the Shadow, overshadowing your Self, inclines you?" "I will do what I will do." "Then, alas, your hour has come." "I care not. I am what I am; no one can take from me myself." "You are not the Self you imagine." "So long as I feel myself what it pleases me to think of myself, I care not. I am content to be myself what I would be. What I choose to seem to myself makes me what I am. My own thought makes me me; my own thought of myself is me. Another shall not make me!" "But another has made you, and can compel you to see what you have made of yourself. You will not be able much longer to look at yourself anything but what he sees you! You will not much longer have satisfaction in the thought of yourself. At this moment you are aware of the coming change!" "No one ever made me. I defy that Power to unmake me from a free woman! You are his slave, and I defy you. You may be able to torture me—I do not know, but you shall not compel me to anything against my will!" "Such a compulsion is without value. But there is a light that goes deeper than the will, a light that lights up the darkness behind it: that light can change your will, can make it truly yours and not another's—not the Shadow's. Into the created can pour itself the creation will, and so redeem it!"[15]

Lilith sets herself up as her own creator and the center of her universe, revealing her turning away from God and towards herself. "Even this sinister personality is redeemed at the end of the fable, further illustrating MacDonald's universalism." Lilith finally sees that to continue in her resistance is to head for complete annihilation. It's because she still has some spark of goodness in her that she is able to reject annihilation.

This dialogue of almost unimaginable resistance portrays, as perhaps few other places in literature, the depths of resistance of a perverse will. As well, MacDonald gives penetrating insights into what fuels such a will to erect, within, the Self as a god. But in the end, Lilith yields.

"I yield," said the Princess. "I cannot hold out. I am defeated." "I will take you to my Father (Adam). You have wronged him worst of the created, therefore he best of the created can help you. "How can HE help me?" "He will forgive you." "I have no power over myself. I am a slave! I acknowledge it. Let me die" "A slave thou are that shall one day be a child. Verily, thou shalt die, but not as thou thinkest. Thou shalt die out of death into life. Now is the Life for that never was against thee!"

In MacDonald's view even the "Shadow himself, because he has the tiny two-dimensional scrap of substance, will eventually enter the house of death and begin the upward journey towards life. "The ultimate redemption of the Shadow reveals the strength of MacDonald's universalism."

To repeat my thesis here: *Lilith is MacDonald's imaginative argument for the inability of any created will to resist the love of God forever. It is thus part of his universalist theology.*

---

[15] *Lilith*, pp. 185-191, *passim.*

The Princess and the Goblin

The Princess and the Goblin emphasizes that evil comes mostly from within our house and not from the outside. This is one of the features of the story that captured Chesterton's attention. And although the goblins in the story may be evil forces outside the persons who live in the upper world, they represent, in my view, "inside realities" in MacDonald's imagery.

So, who might the goblins be? Several "inside" realities in our human existence are possible explanations. They could be personifications of what the Lord enumerated proceed from the heart: "evil thoughts, murder, and adultery.[16] (Recall the "pigs in the mind!") They could be persons in our own households who keep secrets from us because bringing them to light would expose them. (Chesterton thought that secrecy was of the devil.) They could be secret groups or organization in society—fifth columns—that seek to destroy or disrupt that society. We also believe that actual evil spirits can take up unlawful residence in people. And who really knows what other "spirits" may be in the human person? The goblins could mean all these things. All are either inside the person or the various households of society. The story is an argument against the presence of a *supreme* evil force outside of us that is the source of evil. (Even the Great Shadow in *Lilith* is very limited in his influence.)

"Chesterton had found in MacDonald's books a pervasive and almost overpowering evil. But he did learn that it could be defeated; even singing was a weapon against the Kabalds in *The Princess and the Goblins*."[17]

---

[16] Matthew 15:18.

[17] Leo Hetzler, C.S.B. "George A. MacDonald's Myth-Making Powers and G.K. Chesterton," *The Chesterton Review*, Vol. XXVII, Nos. 1 & 2, February/May 2001, pp. 182-191.

So we leave *The Princess* and go on to a brief examination of the devil in one of MacDonald's sermons.

Unspoken Sermons

I will be concentrating now on MacDonald's more studied theological writings, namely, his *Unspoken Sermons*. They contain his more explicit thoughts and teachings not wrapped in poetic imagery. I'll be using his sermon "The Temptation in the Wilderness" (TW) as my main focus.

The first important point to make—which may seem unnecessary—is that MacDonald believed in the devil. Probably a number of "Christian" thinkers and theologians in the 19th century no longer did. MacDonald was not one of them. Speaking of the account of the temptation in Matthew's gospel, he says "the story indubitably gives us to understand that a visible demon came to our Lord." He makes the unusual comment that the kinds of temptations offered by Satan in this account are really foolish! They couldn't possibly be a serious temptation to the Lord. (He is not saying they didn't happen, just that they are—in his view—ridiculous attempts to seduce the Son of God.)

This leads him to ask the question, how could this extraordinary man be enticed? "In the answer to this lies the centre, the essential germ of the whole interpretation: He was not tempted with Evil but with Good; with inferior forms of good. I do not believe that the Son of God could be tempted with evil."

But surely—and this is my view—we weak humans can be, and are, sometimes tempted with evil in all its naked perversity; and we succumb. But perhaps most often it is also some apparent good, or some half-truth. The temptations we saw in *B&C* were apparent truths cloaked in misty rationalizations.

As mentioned, it's an oft-repeated truth that the devil can quote scripture to his advantage. MacDonald has an interesting take on this: "He (the Lord) does not quote scripture for a logical purpose, to confute Satan intellectually, but as giving Satan the reason of his conduct. Satan quotes scripture as a verbal authority; Our Lord meets him with a Scripture by the truth in which he regulates his conduct."

A comment MacDonald made about the temptation of turning stones into bread struck me as something akin to Chesterton's understanding of how the devil works. MacDonald says everything is a word of God, meant to convey God's presence to us. Thus a stone is a word of God, and Jesus would not "alter one word that He [his father] had spoken." MacDonald doesn't use the word "magic," but it was sort of a temptation to become a magician to tempt Christ to turn stones into bread. The devil offers power to do magical things over the forces of nature. Recall Chesterton's point that one of the attraction of the devils is they are practical, they can "get things done" outside the normal course of events. MacDonald saw this as the heart of the second temptation.

One of the great cornerstones of MacDonald's theology is that the true person is one who does the will of the Father. In this sense Christ was the only total person who ever walked on our earth because he did the Father's will perfectly. The second temptation entices the Lord to go against the Father's will by manipulating the elements, showing that he was above the laws of nature. "But he was the Son of God. What was his Father's will? Such was not the divine way of convincing the world of sin, of righteousness, of judgment. It was not the way of the Father's will. It would not fall in with that gradual development of life and history by which the Father works, and which must be the way to breed free, God-loving souls."

MacDonald makes the point that the Lord never used his power for his own sake: "As he refused to make stones bread, so throughout his life he never wrought a miracle to help himself; as he refused to cast himself from the temple to convince Satan or glory visibly in his Sonship, so he steadily refused to give the sign which the human satans demanded, notwithstanding the offer of conviction which they held forth to bribe him to grant." The devil offers power to people for their own aggrandizement, for their own personal spiritual equipment. Jesus never used his power in this way; and he could not be tempted to do so.

The last temptation was similar to the second: Worship Satan and you can accomplish all the good you desire. However, "nothing but the obedience of the Son, the obedience unto the death, the absolute doing of the will of God because it was the truth, could redeem the prisoner, the widow, the orphan, the devouring Pharisee. But it would redeem them by redeeming the conquest-ridden conqueror too, the stripe-giving jailer, the unjust judge." The temptations are always to accomplish "good things" by some easy way, and not by God's way. (We are reminded of all the facile solutions of Professor Lucifer in *B&C*.) And it was when Peter tried to dissuade the Lord from accomplishing his mission according to the Father's plan that the Lord called him Satan.[18]

Finally, a comment by Chesterton brings out the depth of the Lord's identification with us: "In that terrific tale of the Passion there is a distinct emotional suggestion that the author of all things (in some unthinkable way) went not only through agony, but through doubt. In a garden Satan tempted man: and in a garden God tempted God."[19]

---

[18] Matthew 16:23.

[19] *Orthodoxy*, p. 145.

This was not the only source—and certainly not the primary source—of Chesterton's belief that evil will eventually be overpowered. His "Catholic mind" taught him this. C. S. Lewis famously said that MacDonald baptized his imagination. No writer was that significant for Chesterton. But has anyone ever had his mind and imagination so baptized by the Holy Spirit?

AFTERWORD

After reading this book it will come as no surprise if I inform you that I personally believe in the existence of evil spirits. Their existence is attested in the gospels, and belief in evil spirits has always been part of the ancient faith. They *sometimes* tempt us. I emphasize *sometimes* because we have in our human heart a plentiful source of temptation. (Perhaps in the past, before the advent of the psychological sciences, more was ascribed to evil spirits than was warranted.) It takes good discernment to distinguish the source of temptations. The Church teaches that vigilance concerning the *possible* involvement of temptation from evil spirits is part of the normal Christian combat.

To what do they tempt us? Well, to any kind of sin, really, anything that will hurt our relationship with God. But I think they're mostly concerned about our belief in Christ as the Saviour of the world. The demons know who Christ is and that he has won the victory. Their main devilish purpose is to stop belief in Christ from spreading in the world. (Recall the rage of Soloviov's Antichrist when the elders said that their allegiance to Jesus Christ was the most important thing in their lives.)

Who, then, are they most diabolically concerned about? First, the saints, like Anthony and St. John Vianney, the Cure d'Ars, who are famously known for having suffered innumerable attacks from these spirits. Such saints are major threats in the spiritual combat. Every effort has to be made to stop them. The instincts of those demons that attacked Anthony were correct: he went on to become the father of all monks. Their calculations as regards the Cure were accurate also: he became the patron and model of all parish priests. Actually, any formidable Christian leaders such as the Pope, or a Patriarch, or any zealous clergy or laity spreading the name of Christ, would also be high on their satanic lists of concerns.

They are not particularly worried about certain kinds of people, the apathetic, for instance. I recall a story from the desert fathers. A monk went into Alexandria and saw demons just lazily standing around, relaxing, leaning up against walls, not doing much of anything. Then, when he went back to the monastery, he saw demons very, very busy, scurrying around and quite agitated. It was revealed to him that they didn't have any tempting work to do in the city as people were already involved in a great deal of sinful activity. But the monks were resisting all their temptations, and so very concentrated and intense devilish efforts were needed.

Neither do the devils lose any sleep—if they do sleep—over people joining other religions, or make up their own views of reality, as long as they don't believe that Jesus is divine, died and rose from the dead, and that he is now the Lord of lords and King of kings. Any other belief doesn't bother them too much.

What about the "great thinkers" of mankind? Well, the demons don't particularly mind courses in academia on Kant, Nietzsche, Marx, Bacon, Sartre, Freud, Machiavelli, and on and on. Not that these thinkers are all bad. It's just that they don't foster faith in Christ—indeed, some of them help to promote the demons' main project of denying who Christ is. So, many "great thinkers" are not any real threat. They can be classified with the apathetic, not worthy of much attention.

But the demons would be very concerned with courses in secular universities on Aquinas, Newman, Augustine, or the teachings of the popes. So, to my way of Catholic thinking, it would not be anything out of the ordinary to say that the evil spirits would also be very concerned about the teaching of G.K. Chesterton infecting young minds.

Afterword

Of course, it's somewhat of a mystery to Chestertonians, who believe him to be one of the really great *minds* of the 20th century, as to why he is so little studied in universities. However, as with the general "problem of evil," such neglect of Chesterton cannot be understood without also taking into consideration the *possible* involvement of evil spirits. (We saw Origen replying to Celsus that the mystery of evil cannot be understood without belief in evil spirits.)

Now, I'm not implying that all university types who decide that Chesterton should not be studied by the young are all influenced by evil spirits! But I'm saying some might be. This is always a possibility. If I was an evil spirit, I'd certainly be concerned about young people filling their minds with the thoughts of G.K. Chesterton.

Let's imagine a board meeting where courses for the next year are being discussed. And let's envision—and I'm sure this would be a rare occurrence—that somebody suggests a course on the thought of G.K. Chesterton. What would be the main objections? One of them, as Dale Ahlquist points out, is that Chesterton's thought is so comprehensive that he wouldn't fit into any of the academic pigeon holes: "One of the reasons Chesterton is not taught in most of our colleges and universities is that he is not narrow enough to fit into only one of their departments. He is larger than any of the available categories." This would not necessarily be a major obstacle: they could fit him in somewhere if they really wanted to, say, with a course on his poetry.[20] (But even this could be dangerous as it might lead students to want to know more about him and sneak into some library and take out *The Everlasting Man*. I think the bad guys hate this book most of all.)

---

[20] Ahlquist, p. 14.

Nor could such a motion be turned down on the grounds that Chesterton is not a great thinker. He is perhaps the most quoted writer of the 20th century. Nor could there be a legitimate objection to a course on Chesterton because some of the faculty don't agree with his positions on politics, England, 20th century culture, religion, and so on. A University is supposed to be open to examining a variety of thought. They probably don't agree with all of Nietzsche's ideas either; at least I hope they don't. So what's the problem?

Ever since I read it I've been haunted by the remark of Borges which I quoted. He loved Chesterton and got more enjoyment from reading him than from any other author. "But," he said, "it was a pity that he became a Catholic." If a great literary genius and thinker of the 20th century—a favorite of Pope Francis!—could hold such a prejudiced and, yes, small-minded view, it's not surprising that many other intellectuals could as well.

All present day academics, if they are familiar with Chesterton at all, know that he is against all the *isms* of the modern mind. I emphasize "isms." The Church is not against science, but scient*ism*; not against the use of the intellect but against intellectual*ism*; not against a love of country but against national*ism*, not against the feminine but femin*ism*, and so on. Many academics may be in favor of some of these *isms*, believing that they should not only be known but actually become the intellectual *principles* for the young minds of the future. But Chesterton is *agin 'em.*

Chesterton also is especially dangerous to read for Christians who are not Catholic, or for anyone seeking the truth about the Catholic Church. He had the intellectual power to refute all the age-old—I emphasize *age-old*—objections to Catholicism. (He often wished that his opponents would come up with some new objections to make the debates more interesting.) Having courses on Chesterton at secular universities would be too much like having Catholic apologetics courses, and, of course, that is not what a university is for.

One may wonder why I spent time writing on such an esoteric subject as "Chesterton and the Devil"? What does that have to do with the needs of the world? Well, the older I get the more I am absolutely convinced that Chesterton is the greatest Catholic apologist of modern times. He has answered, refuted, given convincing arguments against all the objections to the Catholic faith. This is why he would be—and is—a particular object of attack of evil spirits: they don't want people filling their minds with his irrefutable arguments for Christ and Catholicism. As the greatest apologist of modern times, it is important for people searching for the truth to know that his belief in evil spirits is an essential part of his Catholic apologetics; and how he refuted their lies can assist us in our battles.

In the Preface I made a preposterous connection between Chesterton and the great St. Anthony of the Desert. I concentrated on one aspect of that similarity—Anthony countered the lies of the temptations hurled at him; and Chesterton refuted the lies and falsehoods of the modern world against Christendom, especially in its ancient Catholic form. Anthony could and did influence thousands of people down through the ages. Likewise, Chesterton has influenced thousands of people in modern times. Anyone who has such intellectual power as to turn the face of C.S. Lewis to Christ must be stopped. Anthony had to be stopped. He wasn't. Chesterton wasn't stopped in his own day, but he has been somewhat stopped in the 20th century after his death. But a mini and ever-growing revival has begun in the last century.

I emphasized in this book the apologetic power of Chesterton's mind in refuting falsehoods. It is often said today that *ideas* are not converting people to Christ. There is some truth to this, as

Chesterton himself said: the young people are not interested in the *filioque* and the 29 Articles. However, I still believe that a very substantial number of people need to have their minds enlightened, and are seeking truth. Jacques and Raissa Maritain made a pact to commit suicide if they could not find the truth. Leon Bloy led them to Aquinas who rescued them. Chesterton has probably saved some people from a similar fate.

On the other hand, many people do say, "I don't want ideas. Show me! Show me a gospel way of life, how you live your faith, and then maybe I'll believe."

Here also Chesterton was an apologist: *his life was the greatest argument for the faith*. For years I and many others have been writing about his holiness of life, and "pushing" for a cause for his canonization. While the influence of his writings cannot be over-estimated, we should not forget that he *lived the gospel* in a heroic degree.

This book has been about the place of the devil in Chesterton's pugnacious battle against evil. The devil was one of the objects of his intellectual lance and sword. In conclusion I simply state that *the devil is also fighting against Chesterton*, and continues to do so. This is not making Chesterton a unique subject of diabolical attacks. However, he is one of the very great witnesses to Christ and defenders of the Catholic Church. Anyone who does this is a dangerous threat to Satan's main objective. Thus, Chesterton is one of the outstanding warriors against the lies of Satan, and therefore it is obvious that he would be one of the prime targets of their assaults. He must be stopped!

You may or may not be aware that Pope Francis has been speaking about the devil more than any other pope of the last century, and often in the context of our *battle* with Satan. I choose one of his teachings where he speaks about the need for *discernment* in recognizing the tactics of the devil. Discernment between truth and falsehood was Chesterton's great gift.

Do not these words of the pope words remind us of the ploys of Professor Lucifer in *The Ball and the Cross*?

> It is true that the devil, and St. Paul says so, very often comes dressed up as an angel of light. He likes to imitate the light of Jesus. He makes himself seem good and speaks to us like that, calmly, just as Jesus spoke after fasting in the wilderness: work this miracle 'if you are the son of God, throw yourself down' from the temple! Make a show of it! And he says so in a way that is calm, and thus deceptive.
>
> We should ask the Lord insistently for the wisdom of discernment in order to recognise when it is Jesus who gives us light and when it is the devil himself, disguised as an angel of light. Many believe they live in light but they are in darkness and are unaware of it!"[21]

I emphasize the Pope's present teaching about Satan because it highlights Chesterton's continuing relevance for the modern world: his battle with the father of lies was also an essential part of his own fighting spirit. May this book help you in your own combat; and may it help towards increasing in some small way the stature of Chesterton as one of the greatest of those who jousted with the mills of Satan.

I close with my very first clerihew:

The father of lies,
Most adamantly denies,
This scandalous designation
That hurts his reputation.

---

[21] Rev. Nick Donnelly, *Who Is the Devil: What Pope Francis Says* (The Incorporated Catholic Truth Society: London, 2014), p. 38.